The Rizzlerunk Club

BEST BUDS
UNDER
FROGS

The Rizzlerunk Club

BEST BUDS UNDER FROGS

LESLIE PATRICELLI

CANDLEWICK PRESS

First paperback edition 2021

Library of Congress Catalog Card Number 2013957522
ISBN 978-0-7636-5104-6 (hardcover)
ISBN 978-1-5362-2307-1 (paperback)

21 22 23 24 25 26 TRC 10 9 8 7 6 5 4 3 2 1

Printed in Eagan, MN, USA

This book was typeset in Bulmer.
The illustrations were created digitally.

Candlewick Press
99 Dover Street
Somerville, Massachusetts 02144

visit us at www.candlewick.com

To my best bud, Di

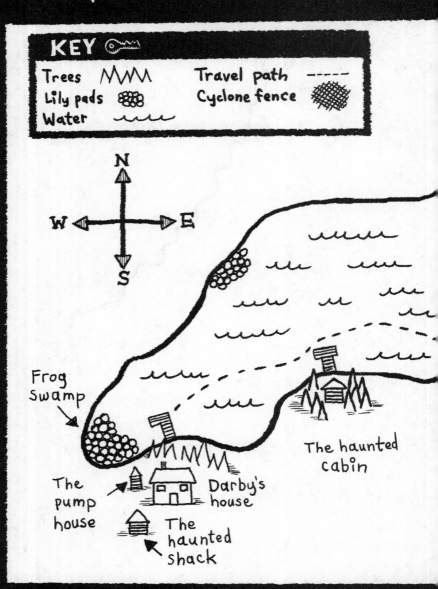

Chapter 1
The Worst First Day

SPLAT.

That is the sound of a partially digested cheese sandwich—*my* partially digested cheese sandwich—hitting the ground between my brand-new tennis shoes, right here in the middle of a game of four square with three girls I just met this morning. Fourth grade, first day, brand-new school, and I'm barfing in front of everyone.

I can hear the kids who could have been my first friends.

"Ewwwwww!"

That's this girl Gabriella. She's the one who invited me to play four square with her. I thought she seemed nice!

"Grooooooss!"

That's Gabriella's friend Tillie, who sat next to me at lunch today—but I'm guessing she won't sit by me tomorrow.

"Look at the new kid!"

That's Mikey Frank. Tillie told me at lunch that he's the cutest boy in school and all the girls have a crush on him, especially Gabriella. He's the worst person to see me throwing up!

Still, I can't stop. I'm bent over, and from between my legs I can see everybody staring at me. Everybody is watching me! This never would've happened at my old school.

Somebody would have helped me.

Why did this have to happen today? I'll tell you why.

This morning my little sister, Abby, who's starting first grade, and I were both feeling sick.

Mom took our temperatures, and since we didn't have fevers, she decided that we were nervous! Well, of course we were nervous. It's our first day at a brand-new school!

Anyway, I knew she was wrong. I'd been nervous before, and this didn't feel like that.

Nervous: Sweaty palms, dry mouth, stomach flips, shaky legs, **FEAR**.

That was nervous. This was sick; seriously stomach-full-of-a-whole-five-pound-gummy-bear sick.

Mom felt our foreheads again. "Nervous butterflies — that's what it is," she decided. "Perfectly understandable. I really think you'll feel better once you get to school and see your new classrooms."

Then there was Dad . . .

Even my dog, Snort, came into the kitchen and barked five times, like, "You. Should. Go. To. School!"

So we ate our eggs and toast (bad idea), grabbed our brand-new fifty-pound backpacks, loaded into Vanna (our minivan), and went. I looked out the window across a pasture, gold and glowing in the morning sun, and this is what I saw: horses, goats, and cows.

We moved from a normal street with a bunch of cats and dogs to the country full of farm animals. The cows smelled, too, which made me feel like barfing. Barfing. Yuck. I hate it. Even thinking about it made me want to . . .

That's when I lost it. I opened my

4

window and threw up my breakfast all over the side of Vanna. When we pulled into the parking lot, I was looking at my new school through a curtain of regurgitated eggs and toast.

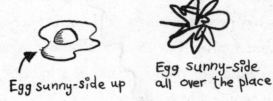

Egg sunny-side up

Egg sunny-side all over the place

"Oh, honey, this is awful!" Mom said. "This is the worst case of nerves I've ever seen. You know you don't have to go to school—though I'd hate for you to have to go through this again tomorrow."

"I'll go," I told her, because I felt a little better having just gotten rid of my breakfast.

"I'll go, too," said Abby, who probably just wanted to get far, far away from Vanna.

So we went.

Mrs. Larson is my new teacher. She seems sort of strict but nice. She asked me if I was feeling okay, and of course I said yes. No one wants to stand out on their first day of school — especially me. That's because I'm shy. Actually, I'm supershy (which sounds like a superhero but isn't because there's no such thing as a supershy superhero). In my old school, being shy wasn't such a big problem, since I'd known everyone since kindergarten, but here I don't know anyone. I had planned to blend in, like the handful of spinach Mom adds to our smoothies.

I did feel better for a little while. But then, during first recess, Gabriella invited me to bounce on this cool springboard thing. I couldn't say no. She might have been my first friend, for all I knew.

After that I felt really bad. I started feeling sick enough that I actually raised my hand in the middle of math in front of everyone (which is a big deal, because supershy people hate interrupting class) and asked Mrs. Larson if I could go to the nurse's office.

Obviously, she let me go. If I were a teacher, I wouldn't want to mop up throw-up.

On the way to the office, I looked around at my new school. Everything was different. My old school was an "experimental alternative" school (that's how parents say "more fun"). We actually had class on the floor in a giant plastic bubble! But then someone spilled their milk in there, and two days later the plastic bubble was gone.

When I got to the office, the office lady brought me to the nurse lady, whose name is (no joke) Mrs. Feverfew. When we walked in, Mrs. Feverfew was taking the temperature of another kid. Abby!

"Hi!" Abby said.

"Hi!" I said.

Mrs. Feverfew looked at us looking at each other.

"We're sisters," I explained. "It's our first day at this school."

"Oh," she said. "I see. Well, first days can certainly be tough."

She put a thermometer under my tongue, then pulled the one out of Abby's mouth and checked it.

"No fever," she said.

"My mom thinkth we're jutht nervouth," I mumbled, trying to keep the thermometer under my tongue. "But I think we're thick."

She took the thermometer out of my mouth. No fever.

nervous

"You know, I'd be willing to guess that you are both suffering from nervous butterflies," Mrs. Feverfew said, like she had already planned this all out with Mom. "I suspect that you'll feel better as the day goes on. Why don't you try going back to class?"

So we went. I made it through geography, then lunch (why did I eat?), then it was recess and Gabriella, Tillie, and another girl, Sonja, invited me to play four square. As soon as I got into my corner and she served the ball, I knew. The worst thing that could ever, ever happen on the first day of school was going to happen. To me.

I will not be sick! I thought. I swallowed. Then . . . my stomach flipped. I took a deep breath. I swallowed again and . . .

I felt better!

I hit the ball back to Gabriella.

What a relief, I almost . . .

So here I am barfing on the four-square court.

And now someone is taking my arm. It's a girl in my class. I think her name is Darby. I noticed her this morning because of her funny glasses and her weird last name. I think it was Dorski, or something like that. (But, then again, my last name is Lattuga, which is extra-super weird. It means lettuce in Italian — which is perfect for us since Mom's so into healthy food. Most of what we eat is lettuce.)

"C'mon, I'll walk you to the nurse," she says, taking me by the arm. "You're Lily, right? I'm Darby."

I barf again.

Then we get to the nurse's office and I do it again. Oh, no! I see barf spots on Darby's new shoes as she hands me off to Mrs. Feverfew. I'm so embarrassed. Darby will never talk to me again, that's for sure.

Mrs. Feverfew seems to believe that I'm sick now, because right away she puts on a doctor's mask, rubs antibacterial stuff on her hands, and calls Mom. While I wait, Abby comes back to the office. A boy is with her, carrying her backpack.

"Abby thwew up in the coatwoom," he says.

Mom arrives in Vanna, which is all sparkling clean, and we're finally going home. At least Mom feels bad. I mean, sure we were nervous about going to a new school, sure we didn't want to go to a new school. But, Mom! Adults can be so dumb sometimes.

P.S. I'm never going to school again!

Chapter 2

Duck Day

Well, I'm going to school again. I tried playing sick to Dad by holding the thermometer up to the lightbulb to make it hot so it looks like I have a fever, but he didn't believe me.

Anyway, Abby and I both feel better. Now Mom's convinced that it was food poisoning.

"You should have told me how bad you actually felt!" she says.

Whatever. I'm glad it's over with, except now I really do have nervous butterflies.

On the way to school, I imagine a magic genie coming out of my backpack and giving me a wish. I know what I'd wish for, because I've wished for the same thing a million times: on shooting stars, birthday candles, and anything else wish-able. I know I shouldn't tell my wish . . . but I will.

I wish I had a shell, like a turtle.

Wouldn't that be cool? Whenever I felt embarrassed or shy or just like being alone, I'd head into my shell. That would be the best part: my shell.

No genie grants my wish, and the next thing I know, I'm back at school. I walk to class slowly, like a turtle, thinking about how everyone is going to be so grossed out by me. In one day, I went from being the New Girl to the Barf Girl.

Eventually, I get to class. I walk in and sit down at my desk and stare at it like it's my favorite book. Maybe if I don't look at anyone, no one will notice me. Then Darby comes over. I don't look up, but I know it's her, because she's wearing the same shoes as yesterday, only they're all cleaned up.

"Hi, Lily, are you feeling better?" she asks.

"Yeah," I say, still looking at her shoes.

"Good, because I only want to see your sandwiches *before* you eat them. That was gross!"

I don't say anything. She stands there for a second, then the bell rings and I watch her feet walk away.

Once everyone is seated, Mrs. Larson turns on her SMART Board and the coolest thing happens! We watch our own school news channel! Even though we didn't have to sit in rows or desks in my old school and we did a lot of art (which I love), we didn't have our own TV station! Mrs. Larson tells me that it's called SHTV for Sunny Hills TV. Everyone starts saying, "Shhh! TV!" and laughing. I guess that's a joke.

There are two kids at the news desk. The boy looks terrified, like he just saw a Sasquatch or something. The girl sitting next to him is wearing a striped sweater, and we can see the backdrop photo of our school through the stripes. She looks like she's cut into layers.

Sasquatch

"Green screen!" everyone shouts.

"Class, that is not necessary," Mrs. Larson says.

We say the Pledge of Allegiance with them, then the girl announces the news. The boy starts to give the weather report, but then he stops and just stares at the camera. The girl elbows him, but he looks too scared to move, so she reads the weather instead. The whole class laughs, even Mrs. Larson. I decide I will never, never, ever do the news.

After SHTV, Mrs. Larson puts on her teacher face and calls roll, then tells us, "Please get out your social studies books and turn to page twenty-eight, and we will read aloud."

How to plead with your eyes. by Lily

1. Tilt head down and look up.
2. Furrow brow.
3. Make sad-happy face.
4. Bat eyelashes.

Oh, no. I hate read-aloud. We're reading about Northwest Native American tribes. I can hardly pronounce Issaquah—the Native American name of my new town! I look up at her, pleading with my eyes.

Please pick someone else, I think. *I'm the new kid!*

I guess Mrs. Larson doesn't have ESP, because she calls on me. I read:

"'Northwest coastal Indian tribes inhabited much of the Pacific Coast, including Alaska, British Columbia, Washington, Oregon, and Northern California. Some of the tribes that inhabited the area were the Salish, Nez Percé, Nis . . . Nisqually, Quinault, Kwak . . . Kwak . . . Kwak . . .'"

"Quack, quack, quack!" shouts Darby.

"Quack, quack!" says Mikey Frank.

Suddenly everyone is quacking like ducks. I can feel my face turn red-hot, like a volcano of embarrassment has just erupted.

QUACK QUACK QUACK

"It's pronounced qua . . . cue . . . tal," Mrs. Larson says. "Kwakiutl."

But it's too late. Everyone is laughing at me. Especially Darby, who sits two rows away. Why does she think *she* can laugh at me? Her bangs hang down so you can't see her eyes, and when you do see them, they look like giant bug eyes because her glasses are so thick.

When it's Darby's turn to read, I draw a picture of her.

I love to draw! It always helps me feel better. In my old school, I was always drawing funny pictures and making my friends laugh, but I don't have any friends to appreciate this one, so I crumple it up and shove it in my pocket.

"Class!" shouts Mrs. Larson. "Please! That is not necessary!"

I've noticed that "not necessary" is something Mrs. Larson says a lot, but it doesn't seem to work very well. Then she threatens to take away recess and everyone gets quiet.

At recess everyone is quacking at me — except for the ones who are teasing me about getting sick. I close my eyes and imagine myself at my old school, on my old playground, with my old friends. I'm sure that I have magically transported myself there, but when I open my eyes, I'm still here: a turtle in a new school, surrounded by ducks.

"Quack!" says a little kid running by with both shoelaces undone. I secretly hope he trips. I know I said the same thing yesterday, but this time I mean it: I'm officially *never* going to school again.

Chapter 3

The Doofus on the Bus

Mom and Dad are always telling Abby and me that we should be empathetic, which means trying to understand how other people feel. Well, guess who's not at all empathetic? Mom and Dad. So, even though I begged to stay home, I'm going to school again.

Even worse, today it's like the first day all over again, because Mom says it's time for us to take the bus! I've never taken a bus to school. At my old school, I walked with Abby and all the

neighborhood kids. Now I won't know anybody.
Plus, sometimes I get carsick. What if I throw up?
I imagine the worst. Then I see Abby.

"You are not wearing that hat to school, are
you?" I ask her.

Abby loves to collect things, like bugs, coins,
rocks, and especially hats — and she wears them
in public! I was hoping to ride the bus unnoticed,
but that's not going to happen if I have to get on
with Abby the mountain girl.

"Oh, it's adorable," Mom says, patting Abby
on the head.

"Hallo, guten Morgen, sprechen Sie Englisch?"
Dad says.

"Hello, good morning, of course I speak
English, Daddy. I'm not German!" Abby says.

When did she learn German? Abby is so

smart. I think she remembers every word she's ever learned. I look at her again. How could she wear that hat? All I ever wear are jeans and sweatshirts. I can't imagine wanting to go to school — especially a new school — in something that no one else will be wearing and everyone will notice. But Abby doesn't care and I guess Mom doesn't either, so we grab our backpacks and head out the door.

"Remember your bus number so you know which bus to get on after school," Mom and Dad yell to us (for the seven millionth time).

We have to cross through the neighbors' yard to get to the bus stop. They have a Doberman pinscher named Zach who barks and growls and looks like he wants to have us for breakfast. He's behind a cyclone fence, but he's still as scary as a great white shark. We run by him.

When I get on the bus, I see a few kids from my class. Gabriella is there, sitting next to Sonja. Tillie is behind them with no one next to her, but all three of their backpacks are on her seat so no one else can sit there. It seems like Gabriella, Sonja, and Tillie are always together, and they don't play with anyone else (except for me on the first day, but I blew that). I hear them laugh at Abby. Then someone quacks at me.

Abby and I find an empty seat near the back, and even though she looks like Gretl from *The Sound of Music,* I'm glad she's here so I can sit next to her.

Once I decide that I'm not going to get carsick, I take out some paper and my favorite pen, which I bring with me everywhere. Like I said, I love to draw. I think I'm pretty good at it, too. I know how to shade and everything. Mom also thinks I'm good. She thinks I might grow up to be a medical illustrator because of the card I made her for Valentine's Day.

favorite pen

For the rest of the bus ride, Abby and I play this game we always play in the car where she tells me what to draw and I try to draw it. She makes it hard.

Draw a Higgs Boson.

Wha?

When we get to school, I stop and look at the number on the side of our bus and memorize it, just like Mom and Dad told me to.

Two hundred eleven. *Two-one-one. Two-one-one*, I say to myself.

I sing it to myself. *Two-one-one*. I sing it more at recess. I sing it in the bathroom. I sing it during math and miss a problem because I accidentally sing it out loud.

But at least I remember the bus number. When

the bell rings to go home, I walk to the bus quickly, since the playground monitor keeps shouting, "Walk, walk, don't run, walk!" The first bus in line has 211 on the side, so I get on. There are lots of kids filling the seats, but I don't recognize any of them. I find the only seat left, then realize it's next to Darby. I don't think she was on the bus this morning. Darby smiles at me — then quacks like a duck. Why can't I get away from her? There's nowhere else to go, so I sit down.

"I didn't know you rode my bus!" she says. "How come I haven't seen you before?"

"It's my first day," I say.

"But you weren't here this morning."

"I rode the bus this morning with my sister . . . but I didn't see you."

"I was here. You weren't," she says. "I would have noticed you. I would have had the whole bus quacking!"

I'm glad that didn't happen. I look around. "I don't see my sister," I say.

"Maybe you're on the wrong bus."

"No. I looked at the number. It's two-one-one. That's my bus number."

"That's the school district number, dummy," she says, laughing. "Not the bus number!"

She grabs me and pulls me up so hard that I fall right down on top of her in the aisle.

"What's going on back there! Get off the floor!" the bus driver shouts.

All the kids start laughing.

"Lily's on the wrong bus!" Darby tells him from underneath me. "We have to get off!" We get up and run down the aisle and out the door. I look up at the side. Duh.

I have no idea which bus is mine. I run toward the first bus in line just as it pulls out. Abby's in the window, waving bye to me. She may look dumb in that hat, but I guess she's smarter than I am.

I feel like I'm going to start crying, but the last thing I want to do is act like a baby in front of all the kids staring out the bus windows at me. Besides, I hate crying in front of anyone. It's like wearing a foofy dress instead of my jeans and sweatshirt.

I turn around and Darby is right behind me. She missed her bus, too. "We're such doofuses!" she says.

I just look at her.

"You know, doofuses . . . like dorks, dweebs, dummies, ding-dongs, dopes . . . duh!"

Like I don't know what a doofus is.

I turn away from her without saying anything and start walking toward the office to call Mom to come and get me.

"Oh!" she says, following me. "I forgot! Of course you're so quiet! You speak duck! QUACK!"

Chapter 4

Hummus Yummus

Now I have to sit here with Darby while I wait for Mom to pick me up from school. I feel like a boiling witches' brew inside: part embarrassed by all the stupid things that I've done, part mad because Darby's the jerk who started everyone quacking at me, and a teensy bit thankful—because she does keep saving me.

"You thought your bus number was the school district number! That just quacks me up," she says.

ARGH! She quacked again!

"Where do you live?" Darby asks me.

"On Pine Lake," I say, waiting for her to quack, because there are lots of ducks on Pine Lake.

"Where on the lake?" she asks.

"That way, at the very end," I say, pointing in the direction of my house.

"Oh. I thought maybe we were neighbors. I live that way at the very end," she tells me. "But that's okay, we could go by boat to each other's houses."

Go to each other's houses?

"But you don't like me," I say quietly, looking at my feet.

"What? Why would you think that?" Darby asks.

"Because you quack at me all the time — and you called me a doofus, and I threw up on your shoes."

"So?" she says. "Everyone throws up some-times. And you're not really a doofus — you're just new here, so you don't know stuff yet. And it's fun to quack! You should try it!"

She looks at me. "Try it!" she says.

"Quack," I say.

"Quack!" she says. "Quack, quack!"

She stands up, waddling in circles, flapping her elbows like a duck. I can't help it. I smile. She sits down again and crowds up against me like we're best friends. "See, it's fun!" she says.

That's when Mom drives up, with Abby — still wearing her Bavarian hat — in the back of Vanna. I try to block the car window so Darby can't see Abby, but the side door slides open.

"Hallo! Sprechen Sie Deutsch?" Abby says.

I jump into the car, hoping to leave before anything else embarrassing happens, but too late. Mom opens the car window. "Aww. Who's this? Have you made a new friend?" Mom asks me.

"I'm Darby!" Darby says.

"Well, hello, Darby!" Mom says. "Are you coming home with us?"

I look at Mom. *What? No!*

"Sure!" Darby says, sliding into the backseat next to Abby. "Can I borrow your cell phone? I just have to call my mom, so she knows where I am."

How is this happening? I thought Darby didn't even like me until about ten minutes ago. And I definitely didn't like her. Now she's coming over and meeting my weird family? She'll never stop teasing me! I hear Darby's mom say yes on the phone, the door slides shut, then Mom starts driving — and talking.

"You didn't eat your spinach for lunch, did you, Abby?" Mom asks her.

Oh, no! Not the spinach thing! Why would she do this in front of Darby?

"YES, I DID!" Abby says, holding her arms up to show off her muscles. "Now I'm super strong!"

Darby looks at me, and I'm sure I look like a tomato. "Did you eat *your* spinach, Lily?" Mom asks.

"MOM!" I say.

"You ate your spinach!" Darby says. "I saw you eat it at lunch!"

"Oh, no!" Mom says, winking at me in the mirror. "Lily, you didn't! Darby, can you please keep an eye on Lily for me? She is absolutely *not* allowed to eat spinach for lunch. It will make her much too strong."

It's this thing Mom has been doing since we were little; she tells us NOT to eat spinach under any circumstances or it will make us much too strong—so we eat it. Of course, now Abby and I know that Mom's using reverse psychology, but we play along. Mom still puts a little bag of spinach in my lunch every day and writes DO NOT EAT! on the plastic bag. I usually hide the bag during lunch, even though I still eat the spinach.

The next thing I know, Darby is following Mom and me into our kitchen.

"I made some snacks!" says Mom. "Veggies with hummus for dipping!"

I groan. Mom is so into healthy food, it drives Abby and me crazy! She even wants to raise our own meat. She's always wanted a pig (which explains why our dog's name is Snort). She thought we'd get a pig and some chickens as soon as we moved out here to the country. There's even an old chicken coop in our yard. But it turns out that the rules have changed, and we live too close to the lake to have any farm animals.

"We're, like, the healthiest family on the planet," I say to Darby. "My dad's a dentist, and my mom's a dental hygienist. Even our last name is a vegetable — it means lettuce in Italian."

"Oh, silly Lily," says Mom, smiling. "This food is good *and* good for you. We're feeding our bodies, not just our mouths!"

I look at Darby, who must think I'm

permanently sunburned, since my face is always turning red. She's already dipping celery sticks into the hummus.

"Yummy!" Darby says. "I've never had hummus before. Hummus is yummus!"

Darby is pretty funny. I have to admit it. Anyway, I'm stuck with her, so I decide to make the best of it. We go down to the lake after our snack and out onto our dock. The sky is filled with cotton-ball clouds, and the water is completely still, except for the trails of ripples behind a couple of ducks. The lake reflects the clouds like a mirror. Darby points toward her house at the other end of the lake, but it's about a mile away — too far away to see.

"Your house is really awesome," says Darby. "And it's new, which means that you probably don't have ghosts."

"Do *you* have ghosts?"

"Of course! My house is the oldest house on the whole lake! It's over a hundred years old. Tons of people have died there. We see their shadows and hear them creaking around. And weird things happen — like doors slamming and other stuff."

"That sounds scary," I say. "But I don't believe in ghosts."

"I can't not believe in them," she says. "My dad's writing a book about true ghost stories. He's even writing about a couple of them that happened in our house!"

"Like what?" I ask, thinking her whole family must either like to make stuff up or be a little crazy.

"Like, my dad was painting my parents' room red, and he left to get a drink of water. When he came back, there were red footprints going up the wall and across the ceiling!"

"Whoa!" I say.

"Yeah. Come to my house sometime and I'll show you some things."

It makes me feel good that she just invited me over, like maybe we could even end up being friends — which would be so weird. Then I imagine going to a spooky one-hundred-year-old house with mysteriously slamming doors and footprints on the ceiling, and my arm hairs start to tickle. Just because I don't believe in ghosts doesn't mean I'm not scared of them.

"Hey! Have you found any frogs around here?" Darby asks me.

"No, but we hear a bullfrog at night. It sounds like a cow, and it's probably as big as a cow, but I've never seen it."

We spend the next hour looking along the shoreline for giant frog footprints, but we can't find any.

"My end of the lake is loaded with frogs," Darby tells me. "I'll have to bring you some next time I come over."

*** *** ***

At dinner, I ask Mom and Dad if they believe in ghosts. "Scientists can explain ghost stories," Abby says.

"That's right, Abby!" Dad says. "Some scientists attribute ghostly phenomena to quantum physics. Do you know what quantum physics is, Lily?"

"I do!" says Abby, and starts explaining quantum physics to Dad, who looks annoyingly proud.

I excuse myself, and no one notices — except for Mom, who reminds me that I have to do the dishes.

When I go to bed, I think about Darby and decide that I'll go to school tomorrow, I guess. I mean, it's not like I have a choice. And anyway, it's been so bad so far — what else could happen?

Chapter 5

Do Not Eat!

When Darby comes into class the next morning, she smiles at me. "That was fun yesterday, Lily," she says. "Your family QUACKS me up!" A few kids quack at me. I look up at her. Why is she teasing me again?

"I mean all you have for snacks at your house is hummus and celery! And QUACKERS!"

Then she starts quacking and flapping her wings like she did yesterday. When no one else was there, it seemed kind of funny. Now it doesn't. I frown. Yesterday I thought we might be friends. I guess I was wrong.

"Class," says Mrs. Larson. "The bell has rung, so sit down and zip those mouths shut. It's time for SHTV."

"Shhh! TV! Shhh! TV!" says Mikey loudly.

"Mikey!" shouts Mrs. Larson. "Shhh!"

"TV!" shouts everyone.

Today it's two different fifth-grade kids announcing the news. They tell us a few items of real news, like about a new exoplanet that could support life and an earthquake in Alaska, then some local sports and the weather (fifty degrees and raining, like usual). Then they tell us the lunch menu, cheeze zombies with tater tots and peas. I love cheeze zombies!

Cheeze zombie

Num num.

Cheese Zombie

At the end of the news, they announce a new contest. Every Monday they are going to introduce a Mystery Kid of the Week. Anyone who wants to guess who

39

it is writes down their answer and gives it to the teacher. On Friday they tell us the Mystery Kid, who gets to go on the news that day and read the sports report. And all the kids who guessed the winner get a roll of Smarties!

"This week's Mystery Kid of the Week," the girl announces, "is a third-grader with curly brown hair. This mystery kid has a brother in fifth grade, loves kittens, and plays baseball."

"I know who that is," David White shouts.

"Hand, David," Mrs. Larson reminds him.

David is always in trouble for not raising his hand before he speaks.

"Children," she says, "if you have a guess as to who the Mystery Kid of the Week is, please write it down on a sheet of paper with your name and bring it to me at first recess. Now, let's take attendance. José Alvero? Iris Barton? Henry Clayton? Darby Dorski? Mikey Frank? Ethan Jackson? Lily Lattuga?"

Before I can say "here," Darby starts quacking, then everyone starts laughing. I should've stayed home today like I'd planned. I don't understand why I have to come here anyway. I love to read and draw and do science projects and play math games on the computer at home. I'm sure I could teach myself everything that Mrs. Larson plans to teach us.

How to teach yourself. by Lily

1. Open textbook.

2. Read. blah blah blah blah blah flip flip

3. Relax. crunch crunch

"Class, please take out a composition book," Mrs. Larson directs us. "For the rest of the year, this book will be your journal for the classroom. In your journal, you may write and draw as you please. Remember, though, I will be reviewing your journals daily, so please use neat hand-writing and be appropriate with your entries. Today I'd like you to write something in your journal that tells me about you."

I decide to write a poem about how I'm feeling. In my old, awesome, creative school, we spent a lot of time learning to write poems about our feelings.

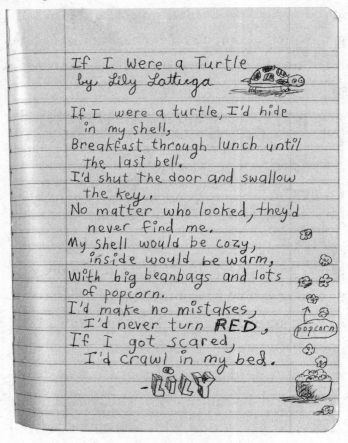

If I Were a Turtle
by Lily Lattirga

If I were a turtle, I'd hide
  in my shell,
Breakfast through lunch until
  the last bell.
I'd shut the door and swallow
  the key,
No matter who looked, they'd
  never find me.
My shell would be cozy,
  inside would be warm,
With big beanbags and lots
  of popcorn.
I'd make no mistakes,
  I'd never turn RED,
If I got scared,
  I'd crawl in my bed.
    —LILY

popcorn

After we write in our journals, we have a spelling test, then go out for recess. I decide to avoid everyone and go to the library.

Iris Barton

Iris Barton is already on a library chair, reading. I don't know why, but no one ever talks to her, and it seems like she's always alone. I think that she spends every recess in the library, which kind of makes sense. Recess wouldn't be so fun without anyone to play with.

"Hi, Lily," she says.

"Hi."

"You can sit next to me."

"Thanks," I say. "I'm looking for a beanbag, though."

Iris seems nice, but there must be a reason that no one is friends with her.

After recess, when I sit at my desk, my chair quacks! I stand up fast. Everyone starts laughing at me — especially Darby, who's laughing so hard that her face is red. I look down and see a little rubber duck on my seat.

"Gotcha!" Darby says. She's still laughing when Mrs. Larson walks up.

"I'll take that!" she says, confiscating the duck and putting it in her desk drawer.

I've never been so glad to have math. Nobody will tease me during math. We're doing multiplication with the number zero.

1000 friends at old school
x   0 friends at new school
─────────────────────────
     = 🙁 friends

But math goes by too fast. The next thing I know, it's time for lunch. I'm the last one in our class to sit down, and the only place is next to Darby. Why does Darby always have an extra seat open next to her? It's like someone used to sit there and now they don't.

I look again to see if I can sit somewhere else, but the benches are full and the lunchroom monitor, who is also the playground monitor, demands that I sit down immediately. I do because she's kind of scary. Her name is Mrs. Rash. She's short and round, with short curly hair that looks like the scouring pad that Mom makes us use to clean super-dirty pans, a red face, and a little bit of a mustache. Everyone calls her Mrs. 'Stache behind her back.

Darby and I are jammed together at the crowded table.

"I got you so good with that rubber duck!" she says, laughing, dumping out her lunch. "Hey! I have a cheese sandwich that looks just like the sandwich you threw up. That was so gross! I could see the cheese and bread and everything. Do you even chew? Oh yeah, of course you don't chew! You're a duck!"

I try to ignore her. It's so weird that I actually had fun with her yesterday. I open my lunch bag to see what Mom packed for me. I don't see much, so I dump it on the table. All that comes out is a plastic sandwich bag with nothing in it — except for a tiny, wilted spinach leaf!

"That's your lunch?" Darby says loudly.

45

Everyone looks. Darby grabs the bag and holds it up so everyone can see it.

I can't believe it. Mom forgot to pack me a new lunch! This is my almost-empty spinach bag from yesterday's lunch.

"Do not eat what?" Mikey asks. "The plastic bag?"

Mrs. 'Stache grabs the bag from Darby. "What's going on here?" she demands. "What is this?"

"My lunch," I mumble.

"This is your lunch?" she says. "This is not a proper lunch!"

Preposterous!

When she says "proper," spit comes out of her mouth. Everyone is looking now. Darby elbows me hard under the table. I'm about to cry, and the elbow jab to my ribs is not helping. Then she kicks my foot. I look down. Darby's cheese sandwich is on my lap. She's saving me! I pick it up and put it on the table in front of me.

"There's her lunch!" Darby says, smiling.

"Is that your lunch?" Mrs. 'Stache says to me.

I look at Mrs. 'Stache. I don't like to lie. If I tell her it's my sandwich, I'm lying.

"I said, is that your LUNCH?"

Everyone is staring at me. I don't know what to do. Darby elbows me again. I nod yes. She sets down the bag and looks at me. I'm not sure what I'm supposed to do now.

"Well, EAT IT, then!" she shouts.

I take a bite, just as someone spills their milk, and she spins around on her heel and starts yelling at them.

Darby bursts out laughing. I start laughing, too. Then Henry Clayton starts laughing, and

Bwahaha! milk comes out of his nose. Everyone is cracking up, and for the rest of lunch, we feel like a big group of friends, just like at my old school.

"Thanks," I say to Darby as we walk to recess.

"You're welcome!" Darby says. "Hey! Let's jump rope!"

We jump rope during the whole recess and it's fun. I don't feel so mad anymore. When I get back from recess, Mrs. Larson has given me an A+ on my poem.

"Lily, this is an excellent poem. I love how you tell me about your emotions. Living inside a shell would be quite lonely, though, don't you think? I'd like to help you come out of your shell more in class!"

To help me come out of my shell, Mrs. Larson calls on me three times before the last bell.

Chapter 6

Insta-Friends

Growing on me

I guess Darby is growing on me.

For one thing, she saved a seat for me every day at lunch for the last two weeks, and I actually liked sitting by her. Plus, I like talking to her, because she tells so many funny stories that make everyone laugh, so now I feel a little bit less shy around everyone. And even though Darby keeps offering me quackers and cheese, I don't care anymore. Now I don't even know why I was so upset about the quacking thing in the first place.

I mean, it was pretty creative — and I'm creative, too. So we have that in common.

Best of all, today is Saturday and she's coming over to my house for the second time! We've decided that we're Insta-Friends. We're thinking that we can sell Insta-Friends boxes on the Internet with nothing in them and get rich!

Darby arrives in her pedal boat, which is about the coolest thing I've ever seen. It's a boat that has bike pedals to make it go! I come down to the lake and meet her on our dock to tie up the boat. I start winding up the rope around the cleat on the dock, but I can't remember how to do it, so Darby shows me. She says it's called a cleat hitch, and she's been tying them since she was zero years old.

She ties it one-handed. In her other hand, she has a brown lunch sack — and it's moving.

"What is that?" I ask.

"I brought you a moving-in present," she tells me. "Look!" She holds open the bag and I look inside.

"Pick it up!" she says.

"Is it safe to touch it?" I ask.

"Of course! Haven't you caught a frog before?"

I reach in the bag and cup it in my hands. It squirms around, tickling me. It's kind of dry feeling, not slimy like I expected.

"It's cute!" I say.

"I know. I love frogs," Darby says. "I named her Rizzlerunk."

"Rizzle what?" I ask.

"Rizzlerunk! She's named after Captain Rizzlerunk. He was the captain of a ship that sunk in the middle of the lake during a huge storm, like a hundred years ago," she tells me.

"What?"

"Captain Rizzlerunk! He crashed his ship into

an island that used to be in the middle of the lake. He hit it so hard that it knocked the top off the island! The top of the island floated to the shore at Pine Lake Park."

"The island floated?" I ask.

"Yeah. You can still see it at the beach there!"

"Darby, islands don't float," I say. "They're the tips of mountains connected to the bottom of the ocean."

"This isn't an ocean," she says. "It's a lake! You sound like you don't believe me, Lily, but it's true. I know because it's one of the ghost stories that my dad is writing about in his book."

"His *true* ghost story book?" I ask, a little bit sarcastically. "My dad says ghost stories can be explained by science."

"So . . . you're a skeptic," Darby says. "Maybe science can explain ghosts, but there's no proof that ghosts don't exist. Come over to my house soon, and I'll show you some stuff that will convince you!"

"Okay."

I cross my fingers behind my back.

"I wish my dad was a writer," I say. "I'd probably be able to eat a lot more candy."

"That's true," Darby says. "But sometimes I'd rather have a dentist dad than a writer dad. My dad's been working on his book forever—like before I was even born! He's not very fun to be around when he's writing. Now he bought a cabin on the lake, away from our house, so he has somewhere quiet to go and work. I don't know why he had four kids if he wanted quiet!"

"Four kids?" I ask her.

"Yep," she says. "We call it the Dorski Zoo."

"Cool," I say. "It sounds fun."

"It's fun," says Darby, "but I wouldn't mind having my own room, like you do. Come on, let's build Rizzlerunk a house so she can have a room! I'm a pro at building frog houses."

I follow Darby while she collects building materials from our bushes. Then we sit down next to the lake.

"Are you glad you moved here?" she asks me, breaking a stick in half.

"Kinda," I say, "but I wish I could live in two places at once. I miss my old room and my old neighborhood and my old friends — especially my best friend, Mary."

"Oh, I know how that feels," Darby says. "I miss my best friend, Jill, too. We were best friends since kindergarten."

"What happened to Jill?" I ask.

"She moved to London last year because of her mom's job."

"That's sad."

"Yeah," Darby agrees. "But if Jill were still here, you might not be my friend. So maybe it's not so bad."

"You mean she wouldn't like me?" I ask.

"No, she'd like you," she says. "But—well—it's hard to explain. Everything would just be different."

"Not to be mean or anything," I say, "but I'm kind of glad that Jill moved."

"That *is* mean!"

Darby smiles and puts the last leaf on the roof of the tiny frog house.

"There! Now Rizzlerunk has a brand-new house, just like you! Only yours is a little bit bigger."

We put Rizzlerunk into her house. She sits for a minute, then hops away. We try to catch her, but she leaps into the lake and starts swimming back toward Darby's end, and neither of us wants to get our shoes wet.

"I hope she comes back," Darby says.

"I guess she misses her old house," I say.

I know how that feels.

Chapter 7
The Haunted Zoo

I can't believe this. I'm going to Darby's haunted house! Mom didn't even ask me first. She just needed somewhere for me to go after school while she went to an appointment, so she called Darby's mom and arranged it. Now I have to go.

"Darby," I say when I see her at school in the morning, "you said your house is a zoo, right?"

"Yep," she says. "The Dorski Zoo!"

Good. I imagine her house filled with zoo animals, instead of ghosts, but I'm still scared.

For the first time since we moved here, I don't want school to end!

It ends.

I follow Darby to her bus (this time on purpose). We sit together near the back. To take my mind off where we're headed, I unzip my backpack and get some pens and paper out so we can draw.

"Want to play heads and bodies?" I ask Darby. "Abby and I play all the time. I'll draw the head, but you have to look away. No peeking. Then I'll fold it over so all you can see is the neck, and you draw the body. When we unfold it, we see what we get."

I draw a weird man's head, then fold it over and hand it to Darby. I look out the window at the passing trees while she draws. When she's done, we unfold the paper and look at it.

"Lily!" Darby says, looking terrified. "This is the ghost

of Captain Rizzlerunk! After his ship sunk, he turned into . . . into . . . this!"

"Very funny," I say.

"It's true! And one night he came out of the lake and crawled to the old pump house in our yard. He left a trail of dead grass — and it's still dead! We think he lives in the pump house. My brothers and sister and I won't go anywhere near it."

I know — well, I think — she's making this up, but it still creeps me out. The bus squeaks to a stop.

"Let's go!" Darby says, grabbing my hand.

The girl who gets off the bus ahead of us looks like a mini Darby, but with frizzy hair — same glasses and everything. She runs ahead, spinning around in circles like a tornado.

"That's my sister, Katy," Darby tells me. "She's in second grade. Do you think she'll spin fast enough to fly away like a helicopter?"

We walk down a long driveway to a really old-looking house. Darby opens the door and steps inside. I

58

stop and look around before I follow her. The house is covered in peeling white paint and lots of cobwebs. It does look haunted. I peek inside. It's dark, but I hear someone singing and dishes clanking, which are normal sounds. I hold my breath for good luck and step inside. There's a bigger version of Darby at the sink — with the same glasses! — doing dishes.

"Mom!" Darby says. "This is Lily, who I told you about!"

"Hi, Lily Who I Told You About!" says her mom, wiping her hands.

"Hi," I say, feeling shy.

I hate meeting new people. I never know what to say to them. But her mom starts talking.

"I'm so happy to meet you, Lily!" she says. "We're all thrilled that Darby's been spending time with you."

"Yeah!" says Katy. "You — and not Jill. Darby's a lot nicer now."

"Dawby nicew!" says a baby voice behind me. I turn around and there's a miniature version

Weewee!

of Katy and Darby and her mom. Same glasses! They must have been on sale or something.

"This is my brother Deke," Darby says. "He just turned three."

"Deke twee!" says Deke.

"Deke, this is Lily," says Darby.

"Hi, Weewee!" says Deke.

Everyone starts laughing. Then Darby opens a cupboard and gets out a box of Pop-Tarts. I can't believe it. Pop-Tarts! Mom would never buy those! We sit down in front of the TV next to Katy and Deke with our snack. This house is so much more fun than mine.

"You get to watch TV on weekdays? You are so lucky!" I say, feeling sorry for myself.

"We don't have as many rules since Daddy moved out!" Katy says.

"Your dad moved?" I ask Darby.

"Mm-hm," she says. "He moved into the writing cabin I was telling you about—just till he finishes his book."

"It's a haunted writing cabin!" says Katy.

"Scaaawy cabin!" says Deke.

I'm not surprised by that.

"C'mon, I'll show you my room," Darby says, pulling me off the couch.

I follow her up a creaky wooden staircase into the bedroom she shares with Katy. She kneels down by her bed and opens a small door to a dusty, dark space filled with boxes. There's a spiderweb inside with a spider in the middle of it.

"That's Charlie," Darby says. "My pet spider! Creepy, huh?"

Creepy, I think, *but not a ghost!*

We sit on her bed, and I look at a bulletin board on the wall, covered in photos of a blond

girl. Darby's in some of the pictures; others look like school portraits. In one portrait, the girl has perfect curly ponytails and is wearing a dark blue sweater with a logo on it, a white button-down shirt — and a necktie!

"Why is that girl in a necktie?" I ask.

"That's Jill!" Darby says. "That's her school picture from London. They all wear uniforms; that's why she's dressed like Harry Potter."

Jill looks like one of those perfect girls who never get dirty. "Do you write to each other?" I ask.

"No, she sent me that photo, but it took forever to get here, and I sort of forgot to write back."

"Sort of forgot?" I ask.

"Well, I guess I didn't want to. I mean, I was sad when she left. I was . . . but now I'm kind of glad. And I get into a lot less trouble."

"Is that why your sister says you're nicer since Jill left?" I ask.

"Yeah. Jill just made me do not-nice stuff."

"Made you?" I ask.

"Well, she didn't make me. It's just — she'd come up with lots of ideas. She made them seem like tons of fun, but they usually turned out to be bad."

"I swear, sometimes she still makes me do naughty things," Darby says. "Like the Ghost of Jill lives in my head."

"She's haunting you from London!" I say.

"Speaking of haunting," she says, pulling me up from the bed, "I'll show you my parents' room."

I imagine bloody red footprints on the ceiling and I get a shiver. But when she opens the door, it just looks like any parents' room. It's all red, but it's more like brick red than blood red.

"Where are the footprints?" I ask her.

"Under the paint," she says. "My parents weren't going to leave them there! Duh!"

I look at her. She must be making this stuff up.

"Now I'll take you somewhere even creepier — if you dare."

"Okay. Fine," I say.

I'm feeling braver. So far this house seems more zoo-like than haunted.

We run outside, across the lawn to a little white shed. The wood looks old and rotten, and the window is cracked. An open rusty padlock hangs on the door. She pushes the door open, and we stumble inside. It's crowded with stuff.

"Check this out," Darby says, pointing to a portrait of a woman. "We call her the Babysitter because she watches you wherever you go. Keep looking at her and walk over there."

I move to the opposite corner of the shed. She is still looking right at me.

"My dad said it was a girl who lived here a long time ago, and she died in this shed! He told me that her bones are inside a big, rusty toolbox."

I look down at my feet.

I scream, running back to Darby, the Babysitter's eyes still watching me. All of a sudden it's dark.

The window is blocked by something. Darby pushes at the door, but it won't budge. We hear a scratching sound.

"A ghost!" Darby says.

She sounds really scared! Suddenly, the door flies open.

A WEREWOLF!

We both scream. I run out the door, past the werewolf, away from the shed, down the lawn toward the lake. There's another tiny shed near the water. I hide behind it. Where's Darby? I look around.

Then I notice it. A trail of dead grass, starting at the shore of the lake and coming right up to me. OH, NO! Captain Rizzlerunk! I'm hiding behind the pump house!

Chapter 8

Of Frogs and Ghosts

I'm frozen behind the pump house. I swear I hear something moving inside. It must be the ghost of Captain Rizzlerunk! I try to get up, but I'm too scared to move. I don't think I've ever been so scared—*ever!*

"Lily! WHERE ARE YOU?" Darby is calling me. I've never felt so relieved. She comes sprinting around the side of the pump house.

"WEREWOLF! Behind me!" she yells. "RUN!"

I stand up and sprint behind Darby along the

path of dead grass. It leads from the pump house to the lake, just like Darby told me! We run onto the dock and leap into the pedal boat. Darby unties us and pushes off.

"RAAARGH!" The werewolf comes to the edge of the dock.

We both scream again. Then the werewolf rips off his mask.

"You jerk, Kyle," yells Darby. "It's my stupid brother!" she tells me.

He looks exactly like Darby but taller — same glasses!

"Gotcha!" he says, smiling and waving.

Darby sticks out her tongue at him.

"You weren't lying!" I say as we pedal away from the dock. "Your house is like a zoo — and a haunted house. It's a Haunted Zoo!"

"I told you," she says.

"Your whole family looks alike, and you all have matching glasses!"

"Yeah. They were on sale."

Darby reaches into a beat-up old cooler that's

tied to the back of the pedal boat and pulls out some life jackets.

"Safety first!" she says, like a super-excited park ranger.

We put them on, then she starts pedaling toward a swampy cove filled with lily pads and cattails. There are a few ducks swimming along the edge of the lily pads, but when we pedal toward them, they flap their wings and skim across the water until they're far away.

"Heeeeere, duck, duck, duck! Heeeeere, duck, duck!" I call them, like Mom does.

"Quack, quack, Kwakiutl," yells Darby.

"Very funny."

I reach up and pet a cattail. It's shaped like a hot dog but feels fuzzy, like it's made of brown felt. Darby picks one and breaks it in half. It's white and cottony on the inside. I look down the long stems of the lily pads. They're like cords that go straight down to the bottom of the

Lily pad cord

lake and plug into the muck. Our boat cuts a path through them.

Suddenly, I spot a little greenish-brown lump on one of the leaves. "Hey, there's a frog!" I say.

Darby pedals toward it, and I reach down and grab it. I pet its back. "I think it's Rizzlerunk!" I tell her.

I hand it to Darby.

"I think you're right! Let's bring her back to your house! Only this time we should bring friends, too. Maybe if she doesn't feel lonely, she won't swim away."

We collect four more frogs and put them in a bucket that Darby keeps on the boat. There are so many frogs that it's easy to find them once we know what we're looking for. Kyle is still sitting on the dock, so Darby yells to him.

"Tell Mom we're going to Lily's house!"

"Did he hear you?" I ask.

Darby shrugs. Her house really isn't very strict! I figure Mom's home by now, so we start pedaling back to my end of the lake.

About halfway to my house, Darby points toward an old cabin. It's tiny, with just two windows and one door. It looks exactly like a face. A scary face. The yard is overgrown with trees and blackberry bushes, so it looks dark even in the daylight.

"That's my dad's cabin!" Darby says. "That's where he's staying while he finishes his book!"

"It does look haunted!" I say, promising myself never to go there.

"Want to go see if he's there?" she asks me.

"I don't think we should leave the frogs in the boat," I say.

Darby points toward the shore again, this time to a humongous house a little farther down the lake.

"That's Jill's house," she says.

"Wow, it's huge," I say.

"It's still their house," she tells me. "Mom told me that they haven't sold it yet."

Suddenly an upstairs window opens wide, then shuts. But no one is there!

"Did you see that?" Darby yells. "Jill is a ghost!"

"I saw it," I say. "But it was probably just a person looking at the house to buy it. Anyway, you have to be dead to be a ghost."

"Maybe she is dead," Darby says.

"No, she's not, Darby. That's ridiculous," I assure her.

But I didn't see anyone at the window either.

We keep pedaling, then Darby points to the shore at Pine Lake Park. There are two giant fir trees growing out of a big slab of dirt. I can see the roots sticking out of the edge of the slab. It looks like a giant picked up the trees from somewhere else and dropped them there.

"There's the top of Captain Rizzlerunk's island!" she says. "I told you it floated to the shore. I'll show you where the bottom of the island is when we get there."

"I'll believe that when I see it," I say.

We keep pedaling. We don't say anything, just look at the sun shining on the water. We see a fish jump. Suddenly Darby points down toward the bottom of the lake.

"See!" she says. "It's shallow! That's the bottom of the island."

I look down and it *is* shallow, maybe only three feet deep, even though we're still far from shore.

"I wouldn't want to swim over that," I say, looking at the algae reaching toward the surface.

"I did once, and something grabbed my ankle," says Darby. "It was probably Captain Rizzlerunk."

"Darby, I know you're making all this up just to scare me," I say.

"No, I'm not! Like my dad always says, 'The truth is stranger than fiction!'"

Finally we get to my dock. I tie up the boat. Now I know how to do a cleat hitch, too! I get our wheelbarrow, and we start collecting sticks, rocks, pinecones, and leaves to make houses for the frogs. We build five tiny little tepees and pick some dandelions to put outside for decorations.

"I wish we could shrink down and live in there!" I say, imagining the inside looking just like my turtle shell.

"Then we could live right next door to each other," says Darby. "That would be so much easier than living all the way across the lake. It's too far to pedal!"

Finally the houses are ready. We go back to the boat to get the frogs. It looks like they're all sleeping now. I guess they got tired from trying to jump out of the bucket. We carry the bucket to shore, then take them out one by one and put them in their new houses. They stay! Then a loud, rumbling sound echoes across the lake.

"The bullfrog!" I say.

All at once, our frogs hop back into the water and start swimming back toward Darby's house.

"Lily," Darby says, "that bullfrog must be huge to make a sound like that! Let's find it!"

We look everywhere along the shore. No bullfrog.

"So you've never seen it?" Darby asks.

"No," I say.

"Has anyone in your family seen it?"

"No."

"Do you know what that means?" she asks.

"No."

"It's a ghost!" she says.

There's a sudden gust of wind. I get a chill down my spine and shiver.

Chapter 9
The Jilly Beans

After listening to the bullfrog through Saturday night, Abby and I spend all of Sunday searching for it, but we don't find it. We even go out in the boat with Mom and Dad at night with flashlights. We can hear it, but we don't see any trace of it.

Mom thinks it must be as big as an elephant to make a noise that loud!

MWAARP.

How'd we miss that?

But if it were that big, wouldn't we be able to find it?

* * *

I tell Darby about our search on Monday morning. "See, I told you it's a ghost!" she says.

"It's not a ghost, Darby," I say. "It's a frog."

"Ghost," she says.

Ribbit

Frog ghost

"Frog," I say—although after seeing the dead grass in front of Darby's pump house and the mysteriously moving window, I don't know what to believe anymore.

"SHTV, everybody!" Mrs. Larson calls.

"SHHH! TV!" everyone shouts.

"Once again, that was not necessary," Mrs. Larson says, raising an eyebrow. We're all quiet for SHTV until they announce the Mystery Kid of the Week.

"The Mystery Kid of the Week," says the announcer, "has a four-year-old brother named Frankie and a cat named Fluffy. He is in fourth grade, got second place in the spelling bee last year, and loves to ride his BMX bike at the pump track."

"It's Mikey!" shouts José Alvero. "I know, because I ride bikes with Mikey, plus I know Frankie and Fluffy!"

"Mikey's brother is named Frankie Frank?" I whisper to Darby.

Then we both get the giggles so bad that Darby pees her pants a little and has to excuse herself to go to the bathroom. Luckily our bathroom is right outside the classroom by the coatroom, so Mrs. Larson is nice about letting us go most of the time. We don't have to get a hall pass like I did at my old school.

I write Mikey Frank's name on a piece of paper and bring it to Mrs. Larson. If Mikey is the Mystery Kid of the Week, it means he has to go on SHTV on Friday. I would never want to be the Mystery Kid of the Week for exactly that reason.

At lunch recess, Darby and I get the last dodgeball out of the bucket to play four square. Gabriella and Sonja are right behind us.

"Now we don't have a ball," Gabriella says.

"Ya snooze, ya lose!" Darby says, which seems kind of mean.

Neither of them has talked to me since the first day of school, but since we have a ball with no partners, and since they are partners with no ball, I decide to really "go out on a limb," as Mom would say.

You can play four square with us.

"What? No! Eww," says Gabriella.

"Yeah, eww," says Sonja.

Gabriella sticks out her tongue at us, grabs Sonja's arm, and walks away. I see them join Tillie by the monkey bars.

"They were so nice to me on the first day of school, and now they're so mean!" I tell Darby.

"Don't worry about the Jilly Beans," Darby says.

"The Whos?"

"The Thems!" Darby says, pointing at them.

"Why are they the Jilly Beans?"

"It's a club," Darby says. "I started it with Jill in second grade. Jill was the president, but it was more like she was the queen because she ruled everybody. Now they still call themselves the Jilly Beans — even after Jill moved!"

"Why aren't you still in the club?"

"I don't know," she says. "They just stopped playing with me. Maybe because Jill was so bossy, they think that I'm the same way. Hey . . . you know what?"

"What?" I ask her.

"I think frogs make better friends than people sometimes. Except you. You're better than a frog."

"Thanks," I say. "You're better than a frog, too."

I watch the Jilly Beans for a minute. They're all standing together playing a clapping game. I've never been in a club. It looks kind of fun.

"Maybe we could join the Jilly Beans together," I say to Darby. "You could just tell them that Jill was the bossy one, but that you and I aren't bossy at all! They'd probably let us in."

"Nah," Darby says. "I don't want to be friends with them anymore. They aren't that nice, and Gabriella's just as bossy as Jill."

"Maybe we should start our own club, then," I say. "We could call it the Rizzlerunk Club!"

"Rizzles sizzle," Darby says, putting her thumb on her butt and making a sizzling sound.

"I've never even been in a club," I say. "What do we do?"

"Well, we need to have an initiation!" she says. "Like eating worms or something."

"I'm not eating worms!"

The bell rings before we can discuss it any further.

worms are yucky.

After school Darby comes home with me, and we plan our initiation. "Okay, so no worms. How about dog food?" Darby says.

I pretend-gag.

"I know!" she says. "I used to play this blind-fold game with Jill. One person got to make a mix of whatever they wanted from the kitchen, and the other person had to eat it without seeing it. Only Jill would always make me go first, and then she wouldn't play anymore! I call going first — but I swear that I'll do my turn."

"You swear?" I ask.

"I swear on Captain Rizzlerunk's grave," she says, crossing her heart.

I find a bandanna in the ski box in the laundry room, and she ties it around my head so I can't see, then starts mixing something. I can hear cabinets opening and shutting.

"Ready or not, here it comes," she says. "Open up!"

First, I taste something really sour like lime juice. Then salt and pepper, then . . . "What is that? Ow!" I yell.

"Tabasco!" says Darby.

I rip off my blindfold and hop around, fanning

my mouth. It's not really that bad, but Darby is laughing so hard that I keep acting. I gulp down a glass of water. "You're the first official member of the Rizzlerunk Club!" she says.

"You're dead," I say, rubbing my hands together. I wrap the blindfold around Darby's eyes.

"Nothing poisonous!" she says.

Now comes the fun part. Darby found stuff in the fridge and the spice cabinets, but she completely forgot about our pantry. Our pantry is filled with nothing but health-food grossness!

weirdest gift ever ↓

Pepper Jelly

I go into the pantry and shut the door. I find red- and green-pepper jellies that someone gave Mom as a gift (weird gift), and mix them in the glass with some pickled-pepper juice. I sniff it—it burns my nose. Perfect! I add honey, a packet of yeast, tomato juice, and three different types of vinegar. Then I stir in some ground coffee, olive oil, fleur de sel (that's fancy salt), and diet tonic water. When I add the tonic water, the whole mixture foams and overflows on the pantry floor. Done!

"You didn't add laundry soap and stuff, did you?" she asks. "I heard you in the laundry room."

"I'm not going to *kill* you, Darby! You're my newest bestest friend! Now open up!"

Darby opens her mouth, and I feed her a spoonful of my concoction. She rips off her blindfold, then her lips get really thin and white.

"Swallow it!" I say.

She swallows it—then she spits on the floor.

"Darby, what are you—"

84

She jumps out of the chair and runs to the bathroom. I follow her. She slams the door. I think she's barfing! I don't go in, and after a while I don't hear anything.

"Are you okay?" I ask her.

"What do you think?" she says.

"I think that you can be president of the Rizzlerunk Club!"

Chapter 10
The Invisible Clubhouse

The next day at school, Darby and I are so excited about the Rizzlerunk Club, we can hardly wait until recess.

"We need to have a clubhouse!" Darby whispers to me. Mrs. Larson raises her eyebrow at Darby.

"We need to have uniforms!" I whisper.

Mrs. Larson raises her eyebrow at me, then instructs us to open our science books to page fifty-eight. It's all about frogs!

Darby and I look at each other and smile. Mrs. Larson asks for someone to read out loud, and Darby raises her hand, all excited. Mrs. Larson calls on her.

"'Frogs use their strong, sticky tongue to catch and swallow food,'" Darby reads. "'Unlike humans, a frog's tongue is not attached at the back of the mouth, but at the front. This allows the frog to stick its tongue out much farther.'"

Immediately, we all start sticking out our tongues, trying to touch the tips of our noses. Mikey can just touch the tip of his nose.

"Mikey wins!" Darby says, then she turns red.

It's obvious that Darby has a big crush on Mikey, and I see Gabriella glare at her. Then Mrs. Larson sticks her tongue way out — and halfway over her nose! "Look, I'm part frog!" she tells us.

Mrs. Larson Frog

Everyone starts cracking up. I love it when teachers act silly.

David has been raising his hand ever since Darby started reading, and Mrs. Larson finally calls on him.

"Did you know that frogs shed their skin every week and then they eat it?"

"My leopard gecko does that!" shouts José.

"Yes," Mrs. Larson says. "There are many similarities and many differences between amphibians and reptiles. Shedding skin and ingesting it is one of the similarities."

Ethan Jackson raises his hand. "Yes, Ethan?"

"I stopped biting my nails, and now I eat the skin around them instead! Does that mean I'm part amphibian?"

"No, Ethan," says Mrs. Larson. "That does not mean that you're part amphibian."

After we read more about frogs, we all get to draw pictures of frogs and write down three of our favorite frog facts. I think my drawing is pretty good, but Mrs. Larson says she was looking for something more realistic, since this is science.

I can't help it. I love to draw cartoons a lot more than I love to draw real things. Cartoons are just more fun, plus they're harder to mess up. If you mess up when you're drawing, you can just turn it into something else. Darby loves to draw almost as much as I do, except she says I'm a lot better than her. (Not to be mean or anything, but it's kind of true.)

Finally first recess comes, and Darby and I run outside. We find a spot in the far corner of our playground by the cyclone fence.

"This is a perfect clubhouse," Darby says.

"How is this a perfect clubhouse?" I ask her. "There's no clubhouse!"

"That's why it's so perfect," she tells me. "It's an invisible clubhouse! This way, no one will ever try to come in!"

She opens the invisible door, steps inside, and sits in the dirt. I sit down next to her.

"Ooh, comfy chairs!" I say, imagining some big, fluffy red velvet chairs.

Then I look toward the four-square court and notice that Gabriella is looking at us. She's saying something to Sonja and Tillie. I feel kind of embarrassed. I might be pretending to be in a big, fluffy chair — but I know we're actually sitting in the dirt. I look at Darby. She doesn't seem embarrassed, or maybe she doesn't notice them.

"The Jilly Beans are looking at us," I tell her. "I think they're laughing at us."

Darby looks up.

"They're looking *behind* us, dummy!" Darby says. "They can't be looking at us. We're in an invisible clubhouse, which makes us invisible!"

Darby just doesn't seem to care what anyone thinks.

"As official president of the Rizzlerunk Club," she says, sitting up straighter, "I, Darby Dorski, will lead our meeting. First on our agenda — the secret handshake!"

We get up and start slapping hands, knocking fists, and bumping hips. High five, low five, bump left hips, bump right hips, bend over, and slap hands. Then Darby puts her thumb on her butt and makes a sizzle sound.

"The Rizzle Sizzle!" Darby says. "It's a perfect way to end the handshake."

"Can Rizzlerunk the frog be our mascot?" I ask her.

"Of course!" says Darby. "Now we need a pledge. Something we have to say every day, like the Pledge of Allegiance."

Darby puts her hand over her heart.

"I pledge allegiance to the Rizzles, of the United Club of Rizzlerunk, and to the invisible clubhouse for which it stands, best buds, under frogs, with loyalty and honesty for all."

We say it together.

Best buds under frogs.

"Now we need uniforms," says Darby. "Something like my friend Jill wears to school in London."

"I'm not wearing a necktie or a skirt!" I say. "What about something easy like a friendship bracelet?"

"No. Everyone has those. But . . . maybe we could make a bracelet out of something else."

Darby pulls her hand out of her coat pocket. It's filled with garbage. Mostly candy wrappers.

"Let's make bracelets out of candy wrappers!" she says. "That's perfect, since candy is the main ingredient for Insta-Friends!"

"We can buy candy after school and make them at my house," I tell her. The bell rings. We jump up to head back to class.

"Oh, wait!" says Darby. "Gotta lock the door!"

She pretends to lock our pretend invisible clubhouse door with a pretend invisible key.

"You're weird," I tell her.

"I know!" she says. "It's fun being me."

"We're going to need a lot of candy to make really cool bracelets," I whisper after we sit down.

My mouth is watering.

"We can get every kind of candy there is!" Darby says. "And we're in luck. My mom gave me a twenty the other day for lunch and forgot to ask for the change, so I'm rich!"

"Mrs. Larson! Mrs. Larson!" says Billy Ditsch, who everyone calls Billy Snitch because he tattles all the time. "Darby's whispering!"

"Billy," says Mrs. Larson firmly, "informing me of Darby's actions is not necessary. You don't need to tell me what other students are doing unless you have good reason."

Then she looks at us.

"Please stop whispering," she whispers.

We can barely keep quiet about our uniform plan until after school.

Chapter 11

Candy Couture

When we get off the bus with Abby, the three of us sprint full-speed past Zach, who jumps at the fence and barks and whines like a crazed coyote.

As soon as we get in the door, I tell Mom that we're doing a project and that we need to go to the store to get lots of candy.

"Nice try," she says. But I convince Mom that it's the wrappers we're after and not the candy and that it's for a creative project. She gives us a look, but then says it's okay to walk up to the store. She even gives me some money.

We're allowed to walk to the Country Store all by ourselves. It's an old, dusty store, so old that it still has horse hitches out front! Not only that, but people still actually hitch their horses up there. Only now they aren't cowboys — they're girls. Lots of girls are into horses out here. They ride horses, talk about horses, and draw horses. I don't like horses that much. I can draw a lot of things, but I cannot draw horses.

At the Country Store, we go straight to the candy racks. We look at every single piece of candy and pick the ones with the best wrappers: tons of Jolly Ranchers, Dubble Bubble, Laffy Taffy, Smarties, Starbursts, and other good stuff.

When we get home, we go into my room with some tape and scissors and get to work unwrapping the candy. Mom brings us a bowl and tells us to put the unwrapped candy into it, and says that we can only have three pieces each.

candy   wrappers

"One for the bowl, one for me," Darby says, popping some Laffy Taffy into her mouth as soon as Mom walks away. Then she pops in another one and another one and another one. I look at her.

"Hey! What about our Rizzlerunk pledge?" I remind her. "'Loyalty and honesty for all.' You invented it!"

"It's a two-person club!" she says, smiling with purple teeth. "We only need to be honest with each other. Get it? Anyway, your mom didn't count the candy, so how will she know?"

Even though Darby is eating the whole time, the bowl still fills up with unwrapped pieces. There's no way she can eat it all. We put all our wrappers into a pile on the bed, like a Mount Everest of candy wrappers. We start cutting and taping and folding and twisting and make these totally cool Rizzlerunk Club bracelets. They even have charms on them! And they say Smarties right on the top, which makes them extra cool.

I put mine on and hold up my arm. "We can never take them off."

"Right," says Darby. "Not even for a bath!"

She holds up her wrist with the bracelet on it. "To Rizzlerunks," she says. "Best buds under frogs!"

Dad calls us for dinner.

"That's what you made with all those wrappers?" Mom asks me, looking at my bracelet.

"Well, there are a lot left," I tell her.

"Is there candy left?" Abby asks.

"A whole bowl," I say, proud of myself for

only eating three pieces. "You can have some — if Darby says it's okay."

I look at Darby, and she just nods yes. Her lips are blue from Jolly Ranchers, and she doesn't eat any dinner. When we're all done, Mom puts a little piece of Darby's chicken on the floor for Snort, but Snort doesn't come.

"Where's Snort?" Dad asks. We all start calling her, but she still doesn't come. I go downstairs to look for her and hear whimpering coming from my bedroom.

"Snort, what's wrong?" I yell down the hall, but as soon as I walk into my room, I see. The candy is almost gone. The rest is spilled out of the bowl all over my bed. It seems like she's whimpering because she feels sick, but then I notice her swinging her nose from side to side and scratching her mouth with her paw.

"Dad!" I call. "Something's wrong with Snort's mouth!" Everyone comes running.

Dad pulls up Snort's lip and shows us her teeth. Her jaw is stuck together with a green Jolly

Rancher. So Dad and Mom carry her upstairs to their bathroom and get to work being a dentist and hygienist. Dad holds Snort and keeps her lips off her teeth while Mom uses one of those pokey metal dental tools to chip away at the candy.

"Good thing you didn't buy chocolate," Dad tells us. "Or Snort might be going to pig-dog heaven."

After Mom and Dad get her mouth unstuck, Mom spends the next half hour brushing Snort's teeth.

Brusha
brusha
brusha

"These bracelets sure take a lot of work!" Darby says to Mom. Mom just looks at us and doesn't say anything.

On Monday, Darby and I both wear our candy-wrapper bracelets to school. When we take off our coats in the coatroom, Gabriella immediately spots them. She walks straight over to me and grabs my wrist like she's my best friend.

"Those are so cool!" she tells us. "I want one!"

"We made them for our club," Darby says. "They're our uniforms."

"What club?" she asks. "You can't have a club!"

"Yes, we can," says Darby.

"Well, I want to be in it, then," she says.

"You can't be in two clubs at once, Gabriella," Darby tells her.

"Fine," Gabriella says. "I was just joking. I wouldn't want to be in your club anyway. What kind of stupid club wears garbage bracelets for a uniform?"

She sticks out her tongue at Darby, then goes to her desk.

The next day, Gabriella and the other Jilly Beans are wearing bracelets just like ours. And by Friday, everyone's wearing candy-wrapper bracelets — even the boys. Mikey was wearing one when he was on SHTV this morning as the Mystery Kid of the Week! And worst of all, everyone is calling them "Gabbys," like she invented them! Darby and I sit in our invisible clubhouse feeling invisible. We take off our Gabbys and put them in our pockets.

"I think we should have invisible uniforms," says Darby. "That way no one can copy them."

"Yeah, I hate copycats," I say.

"Yeah, I hate copycats," Darby repeats.

Chapter 12
Scritch
Scratch

The two kids on SHTV lead us in the Pledge of Allegiance, then read the news. Today one of the kids has a booger hanging from his nose. It's green. It's so big, I'm surprised that it's not acting like a green screen and I can't see the background through his face! I'm distracted by the booger, but then I hear what he's saying.

"This week's Mystery Kid of the Week," he announces, "just started at Sunny Hills at the beginning of this year and made a splash on the playground her first day. She's in fourth grade, has brown hair and brown eyes, loves to draw, and has a sister in first grade."

Darby looks at me and smiles. Oh, no.

"I don't want to be the Mystery Kid of the Week," I whisper. "I don't want to have to go on SHTV on Friday!"

"You're so lucky!" Darby says. "It'll be fun!"

Mrs. Larson tells us to be quiet. I spend the rest of my day worrying about being on SHTV. I'm so worried, I don't even think about the fact that I'm going to the Dorski Haunted Zoo again after school. But I'm not that scared this time anyway.

Dorski Haunted Zoo

* * *

"We should take a bunch more frogs to your end of the lake," Darby says on the bus after school. "Like, fifty frogs. That way, there's no way they'll all leave. Even if your end of the lake is haunted by a giant bullfrog ghost."

"It's not a ghost, Darby!"

"It is too!" she says. "I can feel it! I have my dad's sense for feeling ghosts. He says all of us kids do. But Mom doesn't. She even told me that she thinks my dad's wasting time on his book. But I don't. People need to know about ghosts!"

We get off the bus and sprint through the rain to Darby's house. We eat some Pop-Tarts, then put on raincoats and rubber boots and head to the lake. Darby steers us clear of the pump house, and that's fine with me. I don't ever want to go near that again. I don't care if Captain Rizzlerunk isn't real. The place just freaks me out.

We decide to take the rowboat this time, since it's windy. Darby gets the oars, and we put on life jackets and hop into the boat. She rows us to the swamp. There are plenty of frogs around. They must like the rain. I don't think we'll have any trouble finding fifty of them. We start gathering them up and putting them in the boat.

"This is taking a long time, and it's kind of wet," I say, shivering.

"We're almost there!" Darby says. "Let's count them. One, two, three . . ."

The frogs are hopping all over the bottom of the boat. There's no way we can count them.

"Forty-eight, forty-nine, fifty!" I say. "Close enough, anyway. Let's go to my house. It's cold out here."

Darby rows against the current. We're making progress, but it's slow. The waves are big, so we pretend we're sailors out in a storm. Darby's dad is a sailor, so she's pretty good at it.

"Argh! Look to the leeward! Come about! Come about! Pull in the main sheet! Watch the jib!"

"Aye, aye, Captain!" I yell.

"Lean starboard! Lean port!"

"Aye, aye, Captain!"

The boat rocks dangerously. Darby's getting tired, so I take over the oars, but the wind is getting stronger, and I'm not getting anywhere. We're close to Darby's dad's cabin.

"Let's go see my dad!" Darby says.

Thinking of the haunted cabin makes me row harder, but the wind is blowing us closer to shore. Darby takes over the oars and steers us to the dock. It almost looks like night outside, the clouds are such a dark gray. It definitely looks like night in Darby's dad's yard.

"Why d-don't you j-just go in the c-c-cabin by y-yourself?" I say, shivering.

"You're freezing, Lily," Darby says. "You need to come in. Don't be scared. I've been here before. My dad works here alone all day, so it must be okay."

From the lawn, the cabin face looks especially evil. We walk up some steps to a deck. Some of the boards are broken, and Darby steps over them carefully.

I follow her step by step to the door. She touches the door, and it mysteriously creaks open.

"Dad?" she yells. "Daaaad!"

There's no answer.

"Maybe he's not here," she tells me, "but it's okay to come in and warm up. Come on." I step in through the door. The wind blows it shut behind me and it slams—*BOOM!* Darby and I both scream.

"Darby, I'm scared!" I tell her.

"It's fine," she says.

She takes off her life jacket and coat and lays

them over the old couch. I lay mine down, too. There's a desk in the middle of the small room with an actual typewriter on it.

"Look at this!" Darby says. "It's Dad's book. This must be a new chapter!" Darby starts reading.

" 'Chapter Twelve: The Claws — rough summary. Minnesota, 1986. Patty Jameson, eight years old, was reading quietly on the couch, listening to an angry storm. Her father, Joe, was looking for a flashlight, opening drawers, slamming them shut, cursing that they weren't prepared. Her mother, Dianne, was running water into the kettle to make hot chocolate for Patty. Suddenly — *CRASH* — the lights flickered, then went out. Patty lay in total darkness; complete silence. She called in vain for her mother and father, too afraid to move. Then the noise began: a quiet scratching on the floor near the couch. She called out, "Daddy? Mommy?" but was answered only with scratching. The sound was getting louder, closer to her, when suddenly . . . '

"That's all he's written," Darby says.

"But what happens?" I say. "I need to know!"

"She probably died," Darby says. "Someone usually dies."

"I need the bathroom," I say. "Will you come with me?"

"I'm not staying out here alone!" says Darby.

Darby and I go into a small bathroom with one lightbulb, a dirty toilet, and an old bathtub. She shuts the door.

"Doesn't your dad get scared in here by himself, writing about ghosts all day?" I ask as I sit down on the toilet.

"He told me that being scared inspires him," Darby says.

"I'd be so scared here, I'd be peeing my pants all day instead of writing," I say. We both start cracking up.

Suddenly we hear a faint noise outside the

door. It's a scratching sound! "Shh!" Darby whispers. "Did you hear that?"

There's another scratching sound. It's on the door.

"Hide!" Darby says in a loud whisper. She turns off the lights, and we jump into the bathtub and huddle together. We hear another, longer sound, like claws scratching from the top of the door to the bottom.

Shhh!

"I'm so scared!" I squeak.

"Shh!" Darby warns.

For a moment, it's totally quiet. Then we hear another scratch. The door handle shakes — then turns! We hear another long, loud scratch — and the door bursts open!

Darby and I both scream. The lights go on. "Daddy!" Darby says. "You're so mean!"

I look at her and she's smiling. I'm still shaking.

"Sorry, Darby." He giggles; the bathroom lightbulb sparkles in his eyes. "When I saw the boat, I knew you were here and I just couldn't resist! Hey! Is this Lily?"

"Hi," I say.

"Lily, this is my dad, Doug," says Darby.

"Do you two want some hot chocolate?" he asks us.

He heats up milk on the tiny stove and makes us some cocoa with marshmallows and everything. I guess I thought he would be scary and weird since he's a writer, but actually he's really funny and nice, even though he looks a little like a Sasquatch.

Darby tells him about the frogs in the boat, and how we were taking them to my house when it got too stormy.

"I can tow you over with the motorboat," he suggests.

We put on our raincoats and life jackets and head back outside into the wind. The frogs are still in the boat, sitting in a half inch of rainwater.

Darby and her dad work together to tie our boat to the back of his. He can tie knots even faster than Darby!

"Can we go in our boat, with the frogs?" Darby asks.

"Of course!" Doug says.

We step into our boat with the hopping frogs, and Doug starts the engine and tows us from the dock. We splash down over the waves, which are now whitecaps. Darby and I bounce and laugh every time the boat goes over a wave. We pass by Jill's house and look into her yard. There's a small person in a black raincoat standing on the dock. The hood is up and it looks like the person has no face. Darby grabs my arm.

"Lily! It's . . . it's the Ghost of Jill!"

Chapter 13
The Ghost of Jill

"That is not the Ghost of Jill, Darby!" I say, squinting through the rain.

"It's Jill's raincoat!" Darby says. "And she took it to London with her. I helped her pack it."

"Maybe someone with the same coat moved into her house," I suggest.

"JILL!" Darby calls, but it's too stormy for the person to hear us.

"Dad!" Darby shouts. "It's Jill, over there on her dock!"

Her dad can't hear us in the wind, either, and keeps motoring along.

We watch as the small person turns and slowly walks off the dock, then completely disappears into the fog and rain.

"That just proves ghosts are real!" Darby says.

"It wasn't a ghost, Darby. It was just a person," I say.

But I'm not so sure; I saw it, too, and I saw it disappear.

Doug unties the rowboat at our dock and helps us tie it up. Darby tells him about seeing the Ghost of Jill. He smiles and winks at us.

"Sounds like a good ghost story!" he says. "You should write a book." He gets back into his boat and starts up his motor.

"Better get back before the thunder and lightning start. Bye, honey!" He waves as he drives away. "Bye, Lily, see you again soon!"

"Let's get the frogs out of the boat," I say.

We get a bucket and start putting the frogs into it, then releasing them along the shore. It takes several trips to get them all.

"They won't want to leave your house now," Darby says. "Not in this storm!"

Suddenly, the wind stops. It's weirdly quiet. Then we hear a croak—a very loud croak.

MWAARP!

There's a big splash near the opposite shore—as big as if Snort had jumped into the lake.

"The bullfrog!" I say.

"You mean the ghost frog!" says Darby.

Plunk! Plunk! Plunk! One by one, our fifty frogs start hopping into the water and swimming toward Darby's end of the lake. Darby and I turn and run toward my house, away from all of the ghosts.

The next morning in the coatroom, Darby won't stop talking about the Ghost of Jill.

"You saw her, right, Lily?"

"I think so," I say, "but it was so rainy, it was hard to see. Maybe we were imagining it."

"No," Darby says, "we wouldn't have imagined the exact same thing! It was the Ghost of Jill — I know it was!"

We turn around to go into class, and there it is — standing outside the window, looking in at us, in the same raincoat, rain pouring down.

"The . . . the G-Ghost of Jill!" Darby yells. "Do you see it?"

"I see it!" I say. "Weird!"

The ghost slowly reaches its hand out, then swings open the door. "Daaarbeeeee!" she says.

Darby turns and runs into the classroom, and I'm left staring at the Ghost of Jill. It looks right past me.

"Darby!" it says again. "It's me! I'm back from London!"

Chapter 14

'Ello!

I follow it into our classroom. Darby is at her desk with her arms over her head. Mrs. Larson is working on something. Then she stops, looks up, and smiles.

"Jill!" she says. "It's so nice to see you back here at Sunny Hills!" Then I realize it's not the Ghost of Jill. It *is* Jill!

I tap Darby on the back, but she won't raise her head. The rest of the class is coming in, and everyone is gathering around Jill. I guess no one knew she was coming back except Mrs. Larson.

"Darby," I say into her ear, "it's not the Ghost of Jill—it is Jill! She's back. Darby!"

Darby finally looks up. Jill smiles at her and waves.

With a strong British accent, she says, "'Ello, Darby! I haven't seen you in ages!"

"Jill?"

Jill smiles at her, then turns and goes into the coatroom to hang up her wet raincoat. When she walks back into the classroom, it's like the photo I saw come to life: perfect blond pigtails, navy blue school uniform and all.

With her accent, Jill says, "It would be brilliant if I could sit by Darby, Mrs. Larson."

Brilliant!

"I have a seat saved for you, right here in the front row," Mrs. Larson tells Jill.

Jill gives Darby a sad face, and I feel a little bit jealous. I can't believe Darby's best friend is back. What's going to happen to Darby and me? And to the Rizzlerunk Club? I can hardly hear my own thoughts, it's so loud. Everyone wants to talk to Jill at once, but when SHTV comes on, they all settle down.

"And . . . don't forget to guess our Mystery Kid of the Week!" the announcer says.

"Everyone knows it's Lily!" Mikey shouts.

"Who's Lily?" asks Jill.

Darby points at me. I can tell I'm bright red. This whole Mystery Kid thing is my worst nightmare. It's Wednesday already, and I'm going to have to go on SHTV on Friday. I'm thinking about pretending to be sick, but I already know that doesn't work very well with Mom and Dad.

"'Ello, Lily!" Jill says. "Lovely to meet you."

"For those of you who don't know her," says Mrs. Larson, "this is Jill Johnson. She left us last year to move to London, but circumstances have brought her family back, and we are happy to have Jill join our class."

Clearly everyone but me knows Jill.

We open our math books and start working

quietly on fractions. Then Darby passes me a note. I open it. It says:

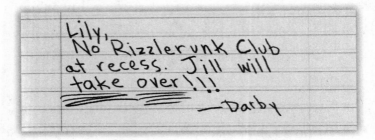

Lily,
No Rizzlerunk Club at recess. Jill will take over!!!
—Darby

I tuck the note away and work more on my fractions. I don't know what to think about this.

$$\frac{Jill}{Darby} + \frac{Lily}{Darby} = \frac{Jillily}{Darby} \ddot\frown$$

It's confusing. The bell rings for first recess.

Jill grabs Darby's arm and says in her silly accent, "Let's go play with the Jilly Beans! It will be so lovely to be back together!"

"You have an accent already?" Darby asks. "In eight months?" She stops Jill so I can catch up.

"British accents are simply contagious!"

Jill says. "Oh, Darby, I've so much to tell you! London was just brilliant! I had ever so many lovely friends. It's too bad Mummy had to move back to her dull Seattle office, and we had to move house again. We really expected to stay there permanently."

"Mummy?" Darby says, then she gets a sad look on her face. "Jill, why didn't you tell me you were coming back?"

"I wanted it to be a surprise!" Jill says. "Plus, Mummy didn't know it would happen. It was really fast. All of a sudden we had to pack up and leave."

I feel completely awkward standing there.

"Oh, yeah," Darby says, pointing to me. "This is Lily, my new friend. She moved here at the beginning of the year."

Jill looks me up and down.

"*Brilliant* unibrow," she says.

I stand there.

"Come, Darby," Jill says. "Let's go play with Gabriella and the rest of the Jilly Beans!"

"Um . . ." Darby says. "Okay. Come on, Lily."
We follow Jill. Darby looks at me.

"It'll be fine," she says.

When we get there, the Jilly Beans are playing four square with three people. Jill says, "Darby and I play winners!"

Gabriella catches the ball.

"Lovely catch, Gabby," Jill says, "but you bodged it. In a proper game of four square, you don't catch the ball! You're out. Darby, shall we?"

Darby and Jill step into the four-square court, and I stand by Gabriella at the edge. There is what Mom would call an awkward silence.

Jill's words repeat in my head. "Brilliant unibrow."

I know I have a unibrow, but I don't like having it pointed out by a stranger. I feel stupid. I want to go hang out in my turtle shell.

To my relief, the bell rings and we go in from recess. But the next thing I know, it's lunch, then lunch recess. It's all the same — Darby, Jill, and the Jilly Beans, with me feeling left out. I decide to go into the library, my safe place, for last recess. I'm reading on the big chair next to Iris when Darby comes in.

"Lily!" she whispers, waving for me to come outside.

Jill is outside the door with Darby.

"Gabriella's being cheeky," Jill tells me, "so I quit the Jilly Beans. Darby says that I can be in the Rizzlerunk Club with you!"

"That's okay, right, Lily?" Darby asks me.

"I guess," I say, looking at Darby.

I thought she said that she didn't want Jill in the club, but I guess she changed her mind— already!

I realize that I'd better try to be friends with Jill. So far I don't like her very much. Mom says you can't judge a book by its cover, but I feel like I already read the cover.

If I could, I might just put this book, unopened, back on the shelf—in London.

Brilliant Unibrow
by Jill Johnson

Chapter 15
Brilliant Unibrow

Darby comes home with me after school, as usual. Now that it's just the two of us again, it feels like nothing's changed.

"I can't believe Jill's back!" I say as we help ourselves to some celery and almond butter.

"I know," says Darby. "I can't believe I didn't *know* she was coming back. We used to know everything about each other."

"Are you happy she's back?" I ask her.

"I guess," she says. "But how could she have

a British accent already? And why did she wear her dumb school uniform?"

"It's kind of weird," I say. "And I kind of don't like what she said about me having a unibrow. I mean, I know I have one. Do you think I have one?"

"Oh, yeah," says Darby. "You have one!"

"Well, I hate it," I admit, "and I don't want it anymore. I want two eyebrows, like everyone else. Except my dad, of course."

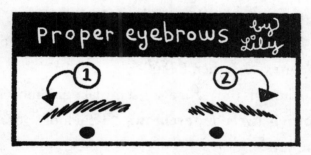

"You could pluck them," Darby says. "That's what my mom does."

"No way. I tried that once. It hurts. But I could shave between them," I say. "I've seen my mom do it!"

I lead Darby into Mom and Dad's bathroom,

open a drawer, and pull out this pink razor thing that Mom says is for ladies. I pick up the razor and turn it on. It starts buzzing.

"Let me see that," Darby says.

She takes the razor and shaves off a bunch of her arm hair. She has a two-inch bald patch on her arm.

"This thing really works!" she says. "Here, I'll do it so you don't mess up. Hold still!"

Darby brings the razor up to my eyebrows. I cross my eyes and try to see it.

"Stop it!" Darby says. "You're squeezing your eyebrows together. Relax!"

She puts the razor against my face and moves it down between my eyebrows. "That looks good!" she says.

I look in the mirror. Now it looks like a uni-brow with a little strip in the middle. "Do some more," I say.

She puts the razor back onto my face and moves it downward. I feel it go right over my closed eyelid onto my cheek.

"Oops," Darby says. "I think I cut off some eyelashes."

I open my eyes and look in the mirror. Half of my right eyebrow and half of my right eyelashes are GONE!

"It was an accident," she says.

"Now what am I going to do?" I ask. "I have to go on SHTV tomorrow!"

"We can fix it!" Darby says. "Don't worry."

She gets some brown eyeliner out of Mom's drawer. "Let me do it," I say, grabbing it out of her hand.

I try to draw in the missing part of my eyebrow, but it looks like crayon. I feel like I'm going to cry.

"Don't get upset, Lily," Darby says. "I have an idea!" She picks up the nail scissors.

"Hold still," she says. "This is totally going to work."

She takes my hair and cuts off a chunk next to my face.

"Now my *hair* looks weird, too!" I shout.

"No, it doesn't," she says. "You can't even tell."

She cuts the hair into pieces about the length of eyebrow hair. "Where's your superglue?"

"Superglue?" I ask.

We find it in the junk drawer in the laundry room, then go back into the bathroom. "Let me do this," I say. "I don't want it to get any worse."

I dab a little superglue at the edge of my eyebrow, then take some of the hair that Darby cut from my head and press it to the superglue.

"That's good!" Darby says.

"Oh, no! My finger's stuck!" I yell. I try to tug it off, but it hurts. Darby tries, and she gets more hair stuck to my face.

"This is so bad! What am I going to do about SHTV?"

"I have an idea," Darby says.

"Oh, great," I say sarcastically. "Because this is a *super* good idea."

Recipe for a **BAD** idea. *by Lily*

superglue + Finger + Forehead + Darby

"We look alike!" she tells me. "I'll go on SHTV instead of you."

"No one's going to fall for that!"

"We can trick them!" Darby says. "We can trade clothes. I'll go in early to be on SHTV, and you go to class and sit at my desk. No one will know the difference since we haven't been on before."

"But my hair's longer than yours," I say.

"That's an easy one!" Darby says. "We'll just cut it."

She sounds so reassuring that I let her cut my hair all the way to my chin, just like hers. I watch it falling to the floor. When I look up, my hair is so shaggy that I look like Snort, and my finger's still stuck to my eyebrow. Now I do start crying. I don't want to tell Mom because I'm so embarrassed, but I decide there's nothing else I can do.

"Mom!" I call.

Mom opens the door to the bathroom. She looks at me, then at the razor, the scissors, and the superglue.

"Lily, your hair! What have you done?"

I cry harder.

"My finger is stuck to my forehead!" I tell her.

"How did you manage that?" she asks me.

"Darby's old best friend Jill came back to school from London, and she said that I have a unibrow, so we decided to shave it, but we accidentally shaved off half my eyebrow. Then we decided to glue some hair onto it to fix it, but when we put the hair on, my finger got stuck to my forehead!"

Mom comes over and gently pulls at my hand. It's stuck.

"Let's get you into the tub," she says.

She fills the tub for me and I get in. I lay my head back into the bubbles and soak my forehead.

Mom leaves the room to call Darby's mom to come and get her, and Darby and I agree on our plan for her to go on SHTV in the morning. Before Darby leaves, she puts on a pair of my sweatpants, my favorite shirt, and my coat, and leaves her clothes behind.

After a while Mom comes in and tries to pull at my finger again, but it still won't come off my forehead. She gets a spatula from the kitchen.

"Lily, you know you are beautiful just the way you are," Mom says, edging the spatula down between my finger and my forehead.

Mom always says stuff like this, and it doesn't help. Well, maybe it helps a little bit.

"You should have asked for help if you were going to use my razor," she continues, "and you should never use superglue without asking."

"I know," I say.

I feel the spatula edge down a little farther. Mom pushes a bit, and my finger pops off of my forehead!

"Thank goodness." Mom sighs.

"How does it look?" I ask her.

She starts laughing.

"Let's fix up that haircut," she says.

I get out of the tub, and Mom wraps me up in a robe and puts a towel around my neck. She lifts up a bunch of my hair and clips it to the top of my head, then starts cutting. When she's done with the first layer, she takes a little bit more hair from the clips and cuts it to the same length.

"How's that?" she asks, combing through my hair.

I examine it. I look like Darby, but I still need

bangs to make it right. "Can you cut bangs?" I ask her.

"Oh, honey," she says. "You know how bad I am at cutting bangs."

"I don't care," I say. "I want them. Besides, they can cover my eyebrows."

Mom brushes a bunch of hair over my face so I look like a hair monster, and starts to clip bangs.

"Below my eyebrows," I remind her.

When she's done, she brushes them straight down. I see right away that they are angled across my forehead all uneven.

"Oh, dear," she says. "Let me straighten those out."

She cuts straight across my forehead, right at my eyebrows. Now they're slanted the other way!

"Mom!" I say. "Can't you cut them straight? I'm NOT going to school tomorrow," I tell her. "Tomorrow is going to be the worst day ever. I have half an eyebrow and my hair looks like a boy's!"

"You'll be fine, Lily. Everything always blows

over. Just try to be confident. You're a great kid. Kids who say mean things usually feel insecure about themselves. The best thing you can do is be nice to them."

Mom always says this, too.

"This wouldn't have happened at my old school, Mom. No one teased me there. I had a lot of friends. I hate that you made me move here."

"It'll get better, Lily. It takes a while to adjust to a new life. It's not easy for me, either. I just have the perspective to know that it will get better."

I don't know why Mom thinks that I don't have perspective. I learned it in art.

Chapter 16

Mystery Kid of the Week

In the morning I try to play sick, but Mom already knows why I don't want to go to school. She might have even let me stay home if she didn't have to work today.

"Let's just put a Band-Aid over your eyebrow," Mom suggests. "You can tell everyone at school you cut your head on a branch or something."

I let her put the Band-Aid on. I look ridiculous.

I get to school wearing Darby's clothes, and I'm just about to walk into class when Darby comes running. She's wearing my clothes, she drew on a unibrow, and she does look kind of like me, except for her glasses.

"Lily! We almost forgot the glasses!" she pants.

She takes them off and hands them to me, then turns around and heads back to SHTV, using her fingers to guide her along the wall. I guess she really can't see without her glasses. I put them on, and now I can't see! I slide them low on my nose like an old lady, walk to Darby's desk, and sit down like we'd planned. I pull the hood of Darby's sweatshirt over my head to hide. A sweatshirt hood isn't as good as a turtle shell, but it will have to do.

When SHTV starts, I can't even listen, I'm so nervous. Finally, they call up the Mystery Kid of the Week.

"And today's Mystery Kid of the Week is . . . Lily Lattuga from Mrs. Larson's fourth-grade class! Lily will read today's sports."

I push the glasses way down on my nose, so I can look at the screen.

Darby is squinting so much that it looks like her eyes are shut.

"Today's sports . . ." she says.

"Hey! That's Darby!" shouts Gabriella. "That's not Lily!"

"Gabriella, shush!" says Mrs. Larson, looking down at her desk and not paying attention.

"Today's sports . . ." says Darby again. "The . . . the . . . Rrr . . . Dang it! I can't read!"

"Move the cue cards closer, Zach," I hear a teacher's voice say from off-camera.

"The Rrrr . . . Ssss . . ." says Darby.

"She's in fourth grade, and she can't even

read!" says the fifth-grader sitting at the news desk next to Darby, laughing.

Suddenly, Darby opens her eyes wide and puts her hand over her heart. What is she doing?

"That's enough, Lily," says a man's voice from off-camera.

"But that's what they sing at football games!" Darby says.

"Thank you to Lily Lattuga, the Mystery Kid of the Week," says the voice. Now everyone in the class is cracking up, and Mrs. Larson is paying attention — and looking at me.

"Lily?" she says. "Lily Lattuga! What kind of

prank are you and Darby trying to pull? Please come to my desk right now."

I take off Darby's glasses and put them on her desk. That's when Darby stumbles into the classroom with her hands out in front of her, like it's pitch-black and she can't see a thing. I hear everyone laughing. They're pointing at me.

"Lily got her hair cut!" says Jill.

"What happened to your face?" shouts Ethan.

"Darby, please get your glasses and come here," Mrs. Larson says.

It's obvious that Darby can't see her desk, so Iris gets up and brings her the glasses. Darby joins me at Mrs. Larson's desk.

"Uh-oh. RTC, here we come," Darby whispers to me.

Darby told me about the RTC because she had to go last year. She says RTC stands for Retraining Center, which is an empty classroom behind the principal's office where they do electroshock therapy to train the bad kids to be good kids. She said that they hook wires all around your

head. Then they make you do the thing that you did wrong—like maybe they'll make me pretend to be Darby, and make Darby sing the national anthem—while they send electricity through your body so you will never do it again. Now that I think about it, I doubt that's exactly true. But still, the thought of it is making my hands sweat, and I wipe them on my jeans.

"What's going on?" says Mrs. Larson.

"Lily cut off half her eyebrow, and she didn't want to go on SHTV," Darby says. "So I wanted to help her by going in her place, but then I messed up."

Mrs. Larson looks at the Band-Aid on my face, and she kind of smiles. "Lily? Is that what happened?" she asks.

"Yes," I say.

"Okay, well, let's not play any more switching games, all right?"

"Okay," we both say.

"You two are quite a pair," says Mrs. Larson. "Now, please take your seats."

Everyone giggles as we sit down. I want to cry. This is the worst day, the worst school, the worst everything ever. Until recess — when things get even worse! Everyone is teasing me on the playground.

"Lily Lattuga can't read! Lily Lattuga can't read!"

Even the kindergartners are laughing at me, and *they* can't read! Then Jill puts her finger and thumb in her mouth and does one of those extremely loud whistles that get everyone's attention. Amazingly, everyone stops and looks at her. Even kids who weren't paying attention in the first place.

Jill starts talking with her silly accent, pronouncing every word slowly. "Leave Lily be, you cheeky little monkeys. Don't you have anything better to do? You're all right idiots. Now go! Get back to your little games!"

Everyone runs away, except for Mrs. 'Stache, who waddles up behind Jill. "What's going on here?" she shouts, spit flying from her mouth.

"Oh, it's just a tiny kerfuffle, Mrs. Rash," Jill tells her sweetly. "No worries." Mrs. 'Stache smiles. I've never seen her do that before.

"Okay, then," she says. "Just have a good recess and stay out of trouble." Wow, Jill can charm anyone!

"Well, enough of that," Darby says. "Come on, Jill. Come see our Rizzlerunk clubhouse. It's invisible!"

"I can hardly see it if it's invisible," Jill says.

But she follows us and pretends to step inside. I sit in the dirt.

"I'm not sitting on my bum in the dirt," Jill says. "I don't want to dirty up my uniform."

Jill's wearing the same uniform she wore yesterday.

"On the topic of uniforms," she says, "the Rizzlerunks need uniforms. Don't you agree?"

"We have uniforms," I tell her. "They're invisible."

"Well, that simply won't do!" Jill says. "You need proper uniforms — like mine!"

"But I like our invisible uniforms," Darby says. "And I'm the president!"

"President?" says Jill. "That's so . . . American. We should have a queen! And since I actually saw Queen Elizabeth in London, I should be the queen. It just makes sense."

Darby looks at her but keeps quiet. I don't know why she's not arguing.

"Right," says Jill. "Now that we've settled that, let's get on with the uniforms. All you need to do is make your parents buy you a uniform like mine. You can get them online. You need a white shirt, blue skirt, blue vest, red tie, long blue socks, and patent leather shoes. Plus you should both grow your hair out. Lily, you look like a boy with short hair. How's your eyebrow, by the way?"

Jill reaches over and pulls off my Band-Aid.

"OW!" I shout.

Jill starts laughing at my eyebrow. Then she drops my Band-Aid in the dirt, and it loses all its stick, so I can't put it back on.

Why is Darby friends with this girl?

Chapter 17

Uniformly Ugly

Neither Darby's nor my parents agree to buy us uniforms, and we can't actually make them do it, like Jill told us to, so we decide to create our own.

After school we go to Darby's house. Jill has horse-riding lessons (English-style riding, of course), so she doesn't get to hang out with us after school. I don't mind that one bit.

$$(Darby + Lily) - Jill = \textbf{PERFECT}$$

After we eat some Pop-Tarts, Darby takes me to her mom's room and goes to her bottom dresser drawer where she keeps all her sewing stuff. She gets some scissors and Darby hands them to me.

"You're right about Jill being bossy," I say.

"I know," she says.

"I can't believe you let her be the queen of our club," I say. "Why did you do that?"

"I don't know," Darby says. "Why did I do that?"

"Maybe you're just used to her being the boss of you," I say.

"No, she's not the boss of me," Darby says. "I decide to do what she says."

"Well, why do you decide to do whatever she says?" I ask.

"I don't know!" Darby says. "It's just easier that way. Okay?" She stands up and opens the closet to her dad's side, which is mostly empty, except for a suit jacket and a few neckties. "Oh, good. He left his ties," Darby says. "Writers don't wear many ties." She picks out a striped tie and a polka dot tie and hands me the striped one.

Then she starts digging through more drawers. She finds a couple of navy blue T-shirts of her dad's that we can make into vests. One says "Paranormal Is the New Normal!" and the other one has a drawing of a wolf on the front.

"I call the wolf!" says Darby.

We cut off the sleeves of both shirts, then cut the collars to make V-necks.

"Now we need skirts," Darby says.

"Can't we just wear jeans?" I ask her. "You know I hate wearing skirts."

"Nope," Darby says. "Not if we're going to look like Jill."

Darby only has two skirts, and neither of them fit her. She chooses the navy blue plaid one with the elastic waistband and gives me the other. Darby's skirt is so short, it shows her legs almost to her underwear. Mine is blue, with little yellow butterflies on it. It's itchy and the waist is too tight. At least it's not frilly, though.

The next day, I call Darby in the morning to make sure that she's going to wear her uniform. Then I get dressed. I have to borrow Mom's long socks, and she only has black argyle knee-highs, so I put those on. My dress shoes are way too small, but I squeeze my feet into them.

"Wow!" Mom says when I come upstairs. "That's an interesting outfit. Look at you in a skirt! I'm not sure about the rest of the outfit, but I like the skirt!"

My perfect uniform →

Oh, no, Mom commented on my skirt twice already. I don't want this kind of attention. I wish I were wearing my turtle shell.

"What does your shirt say?" Dad asks me.

"Paranormal Is the New Normal," I tell him.

"Uh-oh, Lily, are you starting to believe that stuff Darby tells you?" Dad asks. "I heard about what her dad writes. From what I was told, it's hilariously unscientific and not credible by all accounts. I hear he's a nice guy, though!"

"Yeah, he's nice."

"Okay," Dad says. "Just don't believe everything you hear."

At school I feel like I'm wearing nothing. That's how uncomfortable I am. Everyone looks at me when I walk into the classroom.

"Nice outfit," says Sonja.

"It's just like Darby's!" Gabriella says. "Copycats. You guys are trying to look like Jill, aren't you? Well, I don't think you did such a good job! It looks like you bought your outfits at the dump!"

I see Darby already sitting down. Her skirt is so short that I can see a little bit of her underpants. She holds her legs together. When she sees me looking, she puts her jacket over her lap.

Jill comes in next. I can't believe it! She's not wearing her uniform today! She shrugs.

"My darling kitty was napping on my uniform this morning, and I couldn't bear to wake her!" she says.

After SHTV and roll call, Mrs. Larson introduces exponents on the SMART Board. I'm too distracted to pay attention, until Mrs. Larson adds a Superman icon next to the number two. Then she writes a tiny number two on his chest where the "S" should be.

"This is an exponent," she explains. "Exponents have superpowers! For example, in this equation, two to the power of two is four."

"What's so super about that?" asks José.

"Just watch, José, and you'll see," she says, erasing the two on Superman's chest and writing a three in its place.

"Two to the power of three is eight," she tells us.

"NUH-UH!" shouts David. "Two times three is six!"

"That's correct, David. But, this number is an exponent—a supernumber, and it tells us to multiply the two three times." She writes out an equation on the board.

$$2^3 = (2 \times 2) \times 2 = 8$$

"What if it was two to the power of googolplex?" asks José.

"That would be a big, big, BIG number, José," Mrs. Larson says.

Then she asks for a volunteer to come up and write out a new exponent problem on the board. Immediately, I remember what I'm wearing and try to look uninterested, but Darby raises her hand! I would give anything to not go up in front of the classroom any day, and here's Darby volunteering on a day when we're dressed like crazy people. She stands up and everyone starts laughing. Darby doesn't seem to care. She walks to the front of the class. I see Mrs. Larson look at her skirt and raise an eyebrow.

"Darby, lower your arms to your sides, please," Mrs. Larson says.

Darby lowers her arms and looks up at Mrs. Larson, probably remembering the dress code at the same time I do: shorts or skirts have to go below the fingertips. Darby's skirt hem is about wrist-length.

"Oops," she says.

"Darby, you will have to go to the office and find something more appropriate to wear," Mrs. Larson tells her.

When Darby comes back into class, she's wearing some olive-green high-water cords. Jill is laughing so hard, she's crying! I get the feeling she knew exactly what would happen when she told us we had to wear uniforms to school.

"Brilliant trousers!" she says to Darby.

Everyone laughs, including Darby! It's like she doesn't even care what she's wearing! I watch the snap at the top of her pants pop as she sits down. She looks at me and shrugs. I wish I felt that comfortable all the time.

Chapter 18

Funky Bars

Darby and I decide to never wear our uniforms again, but Jill has been wearing hers every day.

"Don't you ever wash your uniform?" I ask her as we sit down in our invisible clubhouse.

"Don't be silly, Lily," she says. "I have five uniforms. One for every day. Mummy and Daddy would go absolutely batty washing clothes every night of the week, and Suzy only comes on Tuesdays and Thursdays."

"Who's Suzy?" I ask.

"Our housemaid," she says, rolling her eyes.

I realize that not only does this mean that Jill lied about her kitty sleeping on her uniform and that she didn't wear hers on purpose to make us look stupid—but also that she could have let us wear one of her extras instead of suggesting that we get our own. She is so sneaky! I'm never going along with one of her ideas again.

"Anyway," she continues, "I've decided that today is the perfect day for our official Rizzlerunk initiation!"

"We already had an initiation," Darby says.

"Rubbish! I wasn't there, so it doesn't count."

"It counts for us," Darby says. "You're the one who needs to have an initiation."

"No, no. We all need a new initiation to make it fair," Jill says. "And I have a brilliant idea for one."

"What?" Darby asks.

"I think our climbing frame is a bit dull . . ."

"Climbing frame?" I ask.

"Right," Jill says. "You call them monkey bars. Anyway, they're a bit dull, don't you think?"

"Monkey bars are fun!" I say.

"I know, but they're the most boring color — beige," Jill says. "But we can fix them! Yesterday I noticed that the janitor's closet door was open all day, and it's open again today. I took a gander inside this morning and guess what I saw?"

"Mops?" I ask.

"Yes, mops," she says, rolling her eyes again. "And loads of paint — in brilliant colors! They must have been used for the mural. So I propose that we make our climbing frame a bit more exciting!"

"You're going to paint it?" I ask her.

"I'm not going to paint it, silly Lily — you are!" Jill says. "You're the artist. You are such a talented painter, I know you'll make it look absolutely brilliant. And have you ever painted anything so big before? Imagine how fun it will be!"

I can't believe that Jill already noticed that I'm

a talented artist! But I'm not going to do it. I said I wouldn't.

"Anyway, since I'm the newest member, I have to do the dangerous job and be on lookout. You get to do the fun job and paint. Plus, I'm the best lookout, because if anyone sees us, I'm a brilliant fibber."

"I don't like to fib," I agree. "And . . . I do love to paint. But, no! We could get in tons of trouble!"

"Plus, everyone at recess is going to see us," Darby says.

"Don't be a twit, Darby. We won't do it at recess," Jill says. "We'll get a library pass during reading and do it then. This is the best idea we've ever had! It'll be fun! Right, Lily?"

I imagine painting cartoon characters all over the bars and nod yes.

Every day before third recess, we have quiet time for reading. That's when Jill raises her hand.

"Yes, Jill," says Mrs. Larson, looking a little annoyed. (It's no secret that Mrs. Larson loves our quiet reading time. It's when she gets to grade papers and fun stuff like that.)

"Mrs. Larson," Jill asks, "may Darby, Lily, and I please go find some new books in the library?"

Immediately, everyone in the classroom besides Darby and me raises their hands. They want to go, too, but Mrs. Larson lifts her eyebrow and gives them a teacher stare. They put their hands down.

Mrs. Larson's eyebrow raise.

"Yes, Jill," Mrs. Larson says. "You may go. Please be on your best behavior. You know the rules: no noise, no messing around in the library. Watch the clock and be back by 1:05."

Mrs. Larson hands Jill a library pass and lets us leave.

I'm feeling extremely nervous. I know that I should turn back. But I'm also feeling excited, like the feeling I get in a haunted house when I don't know what's around the corner but I keep moving ahead. We follow Jill to the janitor's closet, where we see a bunch of small paint cans. Darby and I each pick three colors, then grab brushes and put them into our pockets.

"We need a screwdriver or something to open the cans," I say.

I turn around, and Jill already has one in her hand, along with a mixing stick.

"I just watched my room get painted," she says. "You'd better go, or we're going to run out of time. I'll stand here and keep watch."

Darby and I run as fast as we can to the monkey bars. We wedge the screwdriver under the lid and push down to open each of the paint cans. I look at my brush.

"I thought that we could paint cartoons and stuff," I say. "But these brushes are too wide."

"We can paint stripes!" Darby says.

We start painting turquoise and yellow stripes. There are a lot of bugs and dirt and stuff on the monkey bars, but we paint over it. The paint is drippy, and soon the colors mix together into a pretty shade of green. We cover the ladder, then run to the other side, which we paint pink and orange—but it's not as pretty since our brushes already had green on them.

When the ladders are finished, we decide to do the top of the monkey bars. Suddenly, I realize why people paint the tops of things first. We're getting paint on our shoes from the wet ladders. We rest our paint cans on top of the bars, and then Darby accidentally knocks one over and it falls down to the ground and spills.

"Oops!" she says. "There goes the pink!"

I look at Jill. She's facing the other way, keeping watch.

We both start painting the top, Darby on one

side of the bars, me on the other. I'm painting with bright orange. I love the way it covers the bars when I pull the brush along. We paint until we meet in the middle, then realize that we're trapped on top of the last unpainted bars, surrounded by wet paint.

"Now what?" I ask.

"Let's just paint around each other as much as we can," Darby says. "When we're done, we can jump off."

She starts painting around my shoes. I reach over and start painting around her, too. That's when we hear a terrible, terrible noise.

BRIIIIIING!

"Why's the bell ringing?" I say, looking up.

But I don't have to ask. Kids are running out to recess. In the middle of them, I see Mrs. 'Stache — with Jill!

Mrs. 'Stache marches underneath the monkey bars, then stands, looking up at us. Her face is as red as a dodgeball. It's so red that I can't even see her mustache! Darby and I are as still as ice sculptures. Unfortunately, we're more like melting ice sculptures. A drip of paint falls from my brush onto Mrs. 'Stache's face. She wipes it, leaving an orange streak across her cheek.

BLEEEEEP!

"Wh-what?" she stammers, spit flying from her puffy lips. "What the . . . What the !*@&%!# is going on here?"

Mrs. 'Stache covers her mouth with her hand, her eyes wide. Nobody says a word, until Billy Snitch breaks the silence.

"Did she say '!*@&%!#'?" he asks. "I'm telling!"

He turns to run toward the office, but Mrs. 'Stache grabs his arm.

"Don't you tell on me, Mr. Billy Ditsch, or your recess will never be the same again. Got it?"

Billy nods, terrified. She glares at the other kids.

"The same goes for every single one of you," she says.

All the kids are staring at her with eyes so wide, they look like a bunch of bush babies. Mrs. 'Stache looks back up at Darby and me.

"Get down from there this instant!" she says. We jump. We run. Fast.

"I thought you were watching out for us!" I say to Jill.

"I was!" Jill says. "But I thought it would look dodgy if we were all gone for so long. I was going back to class when the bell rang."

"But you were showing Mrs. 'Stache what we were doing!" Darby says.

"I wasn't!" says Jill. "I was trying to distract her, so you could get away."

"Well, it didn't work," says Darby.

I am so scared to go back to class. I've never been in trouble like this. Not once. I was a good girl — before Jill came back.

I can't believe it, but even though we have dots of paint on our shoes and pants, Mrs. Larson either doesn't see it or ignores it, because she doesn't say anything about the monkey bars. The rest of the day, I expect to be called to the front of the room or sent to the RTC, but we never hear a word about it.

"Well, that's a bit of luck!" Jill says. "I think Mrs. 'Stache didn't tell anyone about what happened because she cursed at you. I suppose she figured that if she tattled on you for painting the bars, you would tattle on her for cursing, and she'd be rumbled!"

"Rumbled?" I ask.

"In trouble," Jill says. "Sorry, it's bonkers how British I've become in such a short time! So . . . Lily, I thought you said you were an artist! The monkey bars look dreadfully messy."

"I think they look like pretty rainbows," says Iris.

"Thanks, Iris," I say.

Jill rolls her eyes.

After school I get on the bus and sit down next to Abby. Suddenly, I realize that I'm not terrified anymore. In fact, I feel as excited as if I just got off a roller coaster. We totally got away with it!

I sit down next to Abby. As the bus pulls away, I look toward the monkey bars. I can't believe my eyes. There's Mrs. 'Stache surrounded by paint cans, holding a paintbrush in her hand! The monkey bars are covered in beautiful flowers with swirling green stems.

I guess Mom's right: you really can't judge a book by its cover.

Chapter 19
Double Trouble

The whole next day at school, everyone is talking about how pretty the monkey bars are. I'm sure that if I'd found a smaller brush like Mrs. 'Stache did, I could have made them look even better.

After school, I get to go to the Dorski Haunted Zoo so Darby and I get on the bus together.

"I can't believe we actually painted the monkey bars!" I say to Darby.

"I know," she says. "We were brave. It feels kind of good, doesn't it?"

"Yeah, but never again," I say. "We were lucky. Now I know what you mean about Jill making you do bad things. She made it sound so fun and easy to get away with! Actually, it was kind of fun, and we did get away with it. But we could have gotten into huge trouble."

"Never again," Darby agrees.

"You know what's weird, though, Darby?" I say. "Even though Jill made me shave off half my eyebrow, wear a skirt to school, and almost get into the worst trouble of my life, I can't help it. I'm starting to like her."

"It happens," Darby says.

After we have some Pop-Tarts, Darby and I decide to pedal to the swamp to look for frogs. The lily pads all have flower buds on them, and we find one of them in bloom.

"Smell this," Darby says, picking it out of the water with the cord still attached.

"Yum!" I say. "It smells like orange sherbet."

"Wait till they all bloom," Darby says. "It's like sherbet heaven."

I start seeing frogs sitting on the lily pads. I'm getting good at spotting them now.

"Look!" Darby points down the stem of a lily pad. "Frogs' eggs!"

I look over the side of the boat and see a big glob of clear jelly stuck around one of the lily pad stems.

"Where are the eggs?" I ask.

"There are clear eggs inside the jelly," Darby says. Then I look up and see something strange.

Frogs' Eggs

"Look at those two frogs," I say, pointing. "They're stuck together. Why are they like that? I've never seen them do that before. Do you think the one on top is hurt or something?"

"I don't know," Darby says.

I pick them up out of the water. I hold the bottom frog in my hand and try to pull the top frog off.

"I can't get them apart."

I pull on the front legs of the top frog and try to pry them off the bottom frog, but they're stuck, like they're superglued. I can't separate them at all.

"Let me try!" Darby says.

She pulls a bit harder than I did, but she can't get them apart either.

"They must be conjoined frog twins!" I say. "You know, like those conjoined twins we saw on TV!"

"You're right!" she says. "Do you think anyone has ever found conjoined frogs before?"

"Maybe we found the first ones in the world," I say.

"Maybe they're worth lots of money!" Darby says.

"Let's go show your mom. She might know what we should do with them. We could be famous!"

I carefully hold the frogs in my hands until we get back to Darby's house. We run into the house.

"Mom! Look! Look!" Darby yells.

"What? What?" her mom says, glancing up from her magazine.

"Look at these frogs! They're stuck together!"

"We think they're conjoined frogs!" I say. "You know, like the conjoined twins on TV. We pulled and pulled on them, and we can't get them apart!"

Her mom looks for a second like she is going to start laughing, which is weird. "What an amazing discovery!" she says. "Maybe they'll want to study them at the University of Washington. Why don't you bring them to Lily's house and show her mom, too!"

"Let's bring them to Jill's house first!" Darby says. "She should be back from riding by now."

We get into the pedal boat and put our frogs in the bucket with some water, leaves, and grass, then steer toward Jill's house.

"What if we get really rich?" Darby says. "Maybe we'll even get to go show the president!"

We tie up the boat to Jill's dock, and I follow Darby up the humongous lawn to the house. I've never been in such a big house before. I feel nervous, but Darby is obviously comfortable. She

Queen Jill's house
(kidding!)

bursts through the deck door into the kitchen.

"Jill!" Darby says. "Jill! Come here!"

Jill comes downstairs.

"Where are your mom and dad?" Darby asks.

"I don't know," Jill says. "I think they're playing cricket or something."

"What's cricket?" I ask.

"Right," Jill says. "I mean golf."

"Come to the lake," Darby says. "We have to show you something."

"Okay, give me a minute," says Jill.

She reaches up and opens a cupboard in the kitchen. "Fancy some biscuits?" she asks us.

"With gravy?" I ask hopefully.

"No, Lily! A biscuit is a cookie in England," Jill tells me. "It would be rank with gravy!"

We eat while Jill puts on her shoes. I look at the photos on a bulletin board. Her parents look like fancy people. Her mom looks just like Jill,

172

with curly blond hair and a shiny smile. It looks like they go to a lot of dress-up parties.

When Jill's ready, we take her to the pedal boat. The two frogs are still in the bucket and still stuck together.

"We found conjoined frogs!" Darby says, picking them up. "We're going to be famous!"

"We tried to pull them apart, but we couldn't," I tell Jill. "They're totally joined together. Have you ever heard of anything like that?"

Jill looks at Darby and me for a second, then smiles.

"No, I haven't heard of *anything* like that!" she says. "You're going to be brilliantly famous for finding them!"

"I know!" I say. "We could be, if they've never been discovered before. We're going to take them to the University of Washington to a frog professor, or call the news."

"Don't be thick!" Jill says. "The frog professor will get famous — not you! And forget the telly. I know how

Frog Professor

to make you even more famous. We can make a video, and I'll share it on Instagram right now. I just joined, but I already have loads of followers. Even some of our friends from school can see it! And, in fact, I might even have a frog professor following me!"

"We can do that?" I ask.

"What are you, daft?" Jill says. "Don't you use Instagram?"

"But how?" Darby asks. "You don't even have a phone."

"I do now!" Jill says. "Mummy bought it for me so she can let me know if she's staying late at work. I can't believe you don't have one yet."

I'm going to have to talk Mom and Dad into buying me a phone. It's getting embarrassing to not have one.

I pick up the frogs and sit next to Darby on the lawn. Jill holds the phone out so we're both in the picture and the lake is in the background. I don't really feel comfortable in front of the camera, especially if the video is going on Instagram, but Darby promises that she'll do all the talking.

"Hello from Pine Lake," says Darby. "I'm Darby Dorski, and this is Lily Lattuga, reporting live with an incredible discovery! Show them, Lily!"

I hold up the frogs in front of our faces.

"Lily and I have discovered real conjoined frog twins! Perhaps the first of their kind in the world! Show them how they're joined together, Lily."

I demonstrate by trying to pull them apart.

"We believe that they are joined chest to back," Darby says. "Do they share the same heart? The same lungs? How do you think they swam as pollywogs, Lily?"

Jill points the camera toward me. I don't know what to say. She told me that I didn't have to talk!

"Um," I say. I can feel my face get hot and am sure I'm turning red. "Maybe like two mermaids wearing one bathing suit top?"

My top! No! My top!

"Yes! Probably like that!" says Darby, laughing. "Mermaid pollywogs!"

I feel more comfortable now because Darby thinks that I said something funny, so I talk some more.

"We are going to bring our discovery to a frog professor at the University of Washington so they can study them," I say. "We want to share our discovery with the world. But, of course, they will live with us."

"That's all for now," says Darby. "This is Darby Dorski and Lily Lattuga signing off."

"Perfect!" Jill says.

Jill touches the screen a few times. "It's up!" she says.

"Already?"

"Brilliant, isn't it?" she says. "Instant fame!"

Chapter 20
Amplexus-tastic

"That was so fun," Darby says, petting the top of our conjoined frogs.

"I agree," I say. "We should make lots of videos!"

"Let's take the frog twins to your house straightaway," says Jill. "You must be dying to show your family!"

Darby and I pedal to my house, with Jill in the back of the boat. When we get there, we see Abby sitting on the grass next to the lake. She's holding something disgusting.

"What are you doing, Abby?" I ask her. "Is that a banana slug?"

"Yes," she says. "I'm looking at its pneumostome."

"Its numo-what?"

"It's the hole that it breathes out of. Did you know slugs only have one lung?"

"You're such a science nerd, Abby!" I say. "Wait till you see what we found!"

"What?" Abby asks. She sticks her finger over the slug's pneumostome.

"What are you doing?" asks Jill.

"I'm plugging up the pneumostome to see what happens."

"Abby," I say, "if you plug up the hole it breathes out of, you're going to kill it!"

"It can't die, it's my friend," she says, petting the slug and setting it down. "Bye, Sluggie! We can play later! So, what did you find?"

"We found conjoined frog twins!" I say. "We're going to be rich and famous!"

"Really? Can I see?"

We show Abby the frogs in the bucket. She picks up the frogs and turns them around in her hands. Then she starts laughing.

"What's so funny?" I ask her.

"These aren't conjoined frogs," she says.

"Yes, they are!" I tell her. "We tried really hard to pull them apart. They're totally stuck together!"

"Don't they teach you anything in fourth grade?" Abby says. "They're stuck together 'cause they're mating. It's called amplexus." Jill starts cracking up. Darby looks at her.

"Jill!" she says. "Did you know?"

"Don't be thick, Darby," Jill says. "Of course I knew! I went to private school in London, where I actually learned something."

"What about our video!" I say. "Is it still on Instagram?"

"Oh, brilliant!" Jill says. "It already has three hundred and eighty-four likes! Mikey likes it! So do Sonja, Gabriella, Billy, and most of the rest of our class. Plus, a whole bunch of other people."

"Take it *off*, Jill!" I beg her.

"No way!" Jill says. "This is going to make *me* rich and famous."

"That's mean, Jill!" Darby says. "Take it down!"

"No!" Jill says. "Come on, Darby, it's brilliant. Everyone will love it." Darby tries to grab the phone, but Jill runs away.

"Ta-ta!" she says. "I texted Mummy, and she's coming to pick me up." She runs up the hill and down our long driveway toward the road.

"We should *not* have told Jill," I say.

"Oh, well," Darby says. "My mom told me that all publicity is good publicity. She should know, since she's in advertising. Anyway, one good thing could come out of this. The frogs could have babies at your house, and we'd finally have frogs at your end of the lake! They probably can't swim away, since they're stuck together."

We bring the frogs down to a little beach by the shore of the lake. There are a bunch of algae-covered sticks and leaves. A perfect place for having babies. We set the frogs down.

"Make babies, froggies!" we say.

The frogs take a hop into the water and float there. Then they start swimming away—back toward the swamp.

"What's so wrong with my end of the lake?" I shout at the froggies.

"I can't believe they can swim hooked together like that," says Darby. "It's amplexus-tastic!"

The next morning, I dread going to school.

It's obvious from the moment that I get on the bus that *everybody* saw the video. The whole bus starts laughing and clapping.

"I saw you on Instagram," says Gabriella. "It went viral! You must be mortified!"

"You thought those were conjoined frog twins?" Tillie laughs.

"How could you not know?" Sonja says.

"Hey, it's the frog twin!" shouts a first-grade friend of Abby's.

I pull my sweatshirt hood over my head and sit down. Abby is laughing with everyone else, telling anyone who will listen about amplexus. She loves the attention she's getting for having a stupid sister who has a mean friend. Make that ex-friend. What was I thinking letting Jill grow on me? Forget it! I'm not going to be friends with her anymore. I'm sure Darby won't either. Not after this.

When I step off the bus, Billy comes up behind us.

"Frog twins! Frog twins!" he repeats all the way to class.

When I get to the coatroom, Jill is there with three other kids, looking at her phone and laughing. I don't want to go in, but it's not like I have a choice. It's school.

"It's a good job you did that video, Lily!" she says in her stupid British accent. "It's up to one thousand six hundred and two likes! I have ever so many new followers, thanks to you and Darby. Just brilliant!"

"Yeah," I say. "Thanks a lot."

"You aren't cross with me, are you?" she says. "I'm making you famous. Isn't that what you wanted?"

I sit down and pretend to read my library book. I hear everyone's voices get loud again in the coatroom and look up to see that Darby has just walked in and is hanging up her coat. When she turns around, she's laughing with everyone like it's funny! She sits down at her desk and smiles at me like nothing's wrong.

Does Darby know something I don't know? Like, maybe if you act like nothing's wrong — nothing *is* wrong?

$$problem^1 - problem^1 = 0\ problems$$

Chapter 21
The Frog Clog

When SHTV starts, I can't believe my eyes or my ears.

"Three of our students here at Sunny Hills Elementary School are famous on the Internet!" one of the announcers says.

"Darby Dorski and Lily Lattuga, two fourth-graders from Mrs. Larson's class," says the other announcer, "were either being hilarious or actually mistook two mating frogs that they caught in Pine Lake for conjoined frog twins. Jill

Johnson, also from Mrs. Larson's class, posted a video on Instagram, where she now has over a thousand followers — and it went viral!"

Then they play our video! Everyone is cracking up, including Jill, Darby, Mrs. Larson, and . . . ME! All of a sudden, it seems hilarious to me, too. I'm starting to feel kind of cool for being on Instagram. Maybe Darby's right, and all publicity is good publicity! We *are* kind of famous now, which is what we wanted.

"Lily and Darby, how amazing that you discovered amplexus!" Mrs. Larson says, after SHTV. "Your timing couldn't be better. It just so happens that we are making our own frogs' eggs today in science!"

Mrs. Larson tells us about our frog project. She shows us pictures of the eggs, but Darby and I already know what they look like.

"We will be using clear water beads. When we put them in water, they will increase in size and look and feel quite a lot like real frogs' eggs without jeopardizing any real frogs' eggs. You will work in groups of three. Each group will be given a glass Mason jar and take turns filling it with water at the sink. Then you will go to the experiment table, take one spoonful of beads, and add them to your jar."

"Only one spoonful?" José asks.

"One spoonful," she says. "You must have room in your jar for the beads to grow—they will increase to one hundred times their original volume and soak up all of the water in your jar. When you are finished, please label the jar and go back to your desks for a quiet activity. You may read, write in your journals, or work on your math packets. It will take a few hours for the beads to reach their full size, which means that we will continue our science unit after second recess. Now you may form your groups."

"Rizzlerunks in a group!" Jill says, grabbing my arm.

What else am I supposed to do? I'm not quite as mad at Jill now, anyway. Darby joins us. We all go to the experiment table and get a jar, then line up at the sink to fill it with water. Everyone is pushing ahead to get to the water.

"We're first in the queue!" Jill says, pushing toward the sink.

"Order, children!" Mrs. Larson says. "I want you in a queue—a line—that you can all be proud of."

Jill fills our jar with water, then Darby adds a spoonful of beads, and I label it. We put it on the table and go back to our desks to write our hypotheses about how the frogs' eggs we are creating will differ from the frogs' eggs we saw in the pictures. Darby elbows me and passes me a note. I open it. It's from Jill.

Lily,

Mrs. Larson has a lot of beads! There is a huge bag of them under the sink. That gives me a BRILLIANT idea! Let's talk at recess! — Jill

I look up at Jill and she's smiling at me. Another brilliant idea? No way! She probably wants us to take the bags of beads and dump them all over the floor so everyone will be sliding all over them. I am not doing that.

But next thing I know, we're at our invisible clubhouse, doing our secret handshake, saying our pledge, and listening to Jill.

"Did you see all the beads Mrs. Larson has?" Jill asks us.

"No, Jill," I say. "I'm not dumping beads all over the place. I don't want to get into trouble — anyway, someone could get hurt!" Jill looks at me and rolls her eyes.

"Dump the beads all over the place? That's rubbish," Jill says. "My idea is ace! I think we should put all the beads into the toilets — in the boys' loo!"

"What's a 'loo'?" Darby asks.

"Right," says Jill. "I keep forgetting you're not British. 'Loo' is the word we use for bathroom in London."

"But the beads are supposed to grow to one hundred times their original size," I say.

"Exactly!" Jill says. "They'll fill up the toilet bowls, and it will be so brilliant when the boys go to the bathroom. They'll be going on loads of frogs' eggs!"

"What if they clog the toilets?" Darby asks.

"They won't clog the toilets, Darby," Jill says. "They're slippery. They'll just flush right down. This is the best practical joke ever."

"What if Mikey poops on frogs' eggs!" Darby says. We all start laughing — then the bell rings.

When we get back to class, the beads in our jars have grown to the size of peas. They're filling up half the jars already! Everyone gathers around to look. Mikey holds a jar up to his face, and I can see a hundred Mikey faces looking back at me, which I don't mind. Darby might be the one with a crush on him, but I think he's cute, too.

"Back to your desks, people!" Mrs. Larson says. "Please leave the jars and the frogs' eggs alone until it's time for our science unit after second recess."

Some people don't take direction well, though, and later, when Mrs. Larson is turned toward the SMART Board, I watch Sonja get up from her seat and pick up her jar. The jar slips from Sonja's hand and falls to the floor, spilling beads and water everywhere. Before Mrs. Larson even turns around, David and José have jumped from their seats and are picking up the slippery balls and throwing them at each other.

"Seats!" Mrs. Larson yells. "Sonja! I asked you not to touch your jars until our science unit after second recess!"

Sonja starts crying. We all go back to our seats and sit quietly. We don't like it when Mrs. Larson gets mad. Luckily it doesn't happen often.

The lunch bell rings, but no one moves. We know we're all in trouble. I can hear Sonja sniffling. Jill raises her hand.

"I'll clean this rubbish up for you, Mrs.

Larson," she offers. "Lily and Darby can help me. We can eat lunch at our desks when we're done."

Uh-oh.

"Darby and Lily, do you agree to help?" Mrs. Larson says. I'm nodding yes. Why am I nodding yes?

"Everyone else, you may line up for lunch."

Everyone grabs their lunch sacks from the basket by the door and lines up until Mrs. Larson dismisses them. Then she gets some paper towels, a broom, and a dustpan from the utility closet and gives them to us.

"Thank you, girls. I can use a break," she tells us, smiling. "Just throw the beads that you sweep up into the circular file. I will see you after lunch recess."

Circular file

We split up the paper towels and start wiping up the water until Mrs. Larson leaves the room. Jill opens the cabinet under the sink and gets out the two huge plastic bags of beads!

"Let's give it a go!" Jill says.

She hands one bag to me and one to Darby. "Follow me," she says.

I follow. What am I doing? It's like Jill has me on a string or something! We walk into the boys' room.

"Eww, it's rank in here — boys are so gross!" Jill says. Then she points to the urinal. "Hey! Bonus! There's a silly boy toilet in here, too!"

Darby pours half a bag of beads in one toilet and half a bag in the other. Jill plugs the sinks and fills them with water. I pour a bunch of beads into each sink. We try to fill the urinal with water, but it drains, so Jill takes a wad of paper towels, gets it wet, and clogs up the drain. I pour the rest of my bag of beads into the urinal, then we toss the bags in the trash and run back to the classroom to finish cleaning up Sonja's mess.

The beads are difficult to sweep up. We try to pick them up, but they keep shooting out from our fingers across the floor. We throw a few at one another, then realize we'd better hurry, so we work hard until all of them are in the garbage. When we're done, we sit at our desks and eat.

After recess, everyone gathers around the science table. The jars are full to the rim with clear beads. There's no water left.

"We made frogs' eggs!" José shouts.

"Without frogs!" says Mikey.

Darby smiles and looks at me.

"Who needs amplexus, anyway?" she says.

Chapter 22
Strike One

"Everyone into your groups, please," Mrs. Larson tells us. "Find your jar and take it to your desk to fill out your work sheets. I'd like you to observe the beads and see how your observations on their changes match your hypotheses by comparing and contrasting the look and feel of your frogs' eggs to the descriptions of the eggs in your textbooks, and complete your end-of-unit questions."

"Mrs. Larson?" Henry asks loudly. "Can I go to the bathroom?"

"Henry, quietly, please, there's no reason to yell. Yes, you may go."

I look at Darby. She looks terrified; her face has gone completely still. I look at Jill, and I can tell she's trying not to laugh—she's not even scared that we're going to get into trouble.

"MRS. LARSON! MRS. LARSON!" Henry yells from the coatroom through the classroom door.

"Henry," Mrs. Larson says. "As I just said, there is NO reason to yell."

"There IS a reason to yell, Mrs. Larson! There are FROGS in the bathroom!" Henry is standing in the doorway with his pants down at his knees. I can see his underwear.

"Frogs in the bathroom?" Mrs. Larson asks him doubtfully.

"Frogs' EGGS!" Henry yells. "The bathroom is FILLED with FROGS' EGGS!" Mrs. Larson's face goes white, and she gets up from her desk.

"Let's pull up your pants, Henry, and please show me what you are talking about."

As soon as Mrs. Larson leaves the room, Jill gets up and follows her. She signals Darby and me to follow, too, so we do. The rest of the class gathers behind us.

"Pretend like you don't know what's going on!" Jill whispers to us.

We step into the coatroom. There are quite a few frogs' eggs scattered around the floor. Suddenly, we hear a lady's scream from behind the boys' room door. Jill opens the door to the bathroom, and there's Mrs. Larson—on the floor, elbow deep in frogs' eggs.

"She slipped!" Henry says.

Uh-oh. The toilets are overflowing with frogs'

eggs, the urinal is overflowing with frogs' eggs, and the sinks are overflowing with frogs' eggs. The water is on in one of the sinks. We look at Jill.

"Oh, dear," she whispers. "I didn't mean to leave it on!"

Mrs. Larson turns around to look right at us. Without thinking, I pull my sweatshirt hood over my head.

"Who did this?" she says.

"It was Lily and Darby's idea!" Jill says. She starts crying. "I tried to stop them, Mrs. Larson, I did, but they wouldn't listen to reason. They told me it was a brilliant idea!"

I hear Darby start to cry, too. I'm fascinated for just a moment as I watch Mrs. Larson's face cycle through several of my favorite colors of Crayola crayons: Salmon to Raspberry to Red to Brick Red to Maroon.

Mrs. Larson gets to her feet, holding the sink for balance, then comes toward us. The whole class backs up.

"Lily and Darby, is this true?" Mrs. Larson asks us.

I'm too scared to say anything. I guess Darby is, too. But we must look guilty.

"Take your backpacks and go to the principal's office," Mrs. Larson says. "You will not be coming back to class."

Darby and I walk slowly to the office, too scared to even talk to each other. Darby's crying so much, she's hiccupping, but I'm too scared to cry. This is the first time I've ever been sent to the principal's office for doing something bad at school. Darby stops me right outside the office door.

"Don't tell on Jill," she whispers.

"Why?" I ask her. "She told on us!"

"Because, Lily — no one will believe us. All the teachers think she's perfect."

"But her fingerprints are probably all over the bathroom. We could prove it!"

"Even if her fingerprints are everywhere," Darby tells me, "Jill will get out of it — and we'll get into more trouble. Just don't tell, okay?"

"Fine," I say.

We walk into the office, and the office lady, Ms. Amy, tells us to have a seat. I look at the clock and see that school is almost over. I hope that Principal Walker is too busy to see us before the bell rings, and we can just get on the bus and go home. No such luck. Principal Walker walks in and motions for us to follow him. He looks like a giant. He's big and strong with short blond hair. Mom says he reminds her of a professional wrestler on TV. He looks at us like we're his opponents and he's about to slam us to the floor. But when he talks, his voice is kind of high and stuffy, like he has a cold. He doesn't sound as scary as he looks.

"Lily and Darby," Mr. Walker says, "can you please explain to me the choice that you made today?"

"Okay," Darby says, sniffling. "We thought it would be funny for the boys to find frogs' eggs in their toilets. We didn't know that they'd get so big! Then we accidentally left the water on. That's how it got so out of control."

"Is this what happened, Lily?" Mr. Walker asks me.

I nod and swallow. It feels like I have a mouth full of shredded wheat.

"Lily and Darby," Mr. Walker says, blowing his nose, "you made a bad, bad choice today. As a consequence, you will be spending first recess in the RTC over the next week."

Not the RTC!

"In this school, we have a three-strikes-you're-out rule," he continues. "This is strike one for both of you. If you were to get three strikes, you would be suspended, which would be a very serious mark on your school record. You don't want that to happen, do you?"

"No," we both say.

"I will be calling your parents and informing them of your actions," he tells us.

Darby starts crying harder. I feel as if I swallowed a frog.

"Do you have anything else you'd like to tell me?"

It was Jill's fault! I want to say. *You should call Jill's parents — not ours!* "Ji—" I start.

But I stop. I know Darby's right; Jill would talk her way out of it, and I'd probably just get into more trouble for trying to blame her.

We hear the last bell ring, and Mr. Walker excuses us to catch our buses. We have to run.

I'm nervous the whole way home on the bus. I think about running away, but I don't have my toothbrush, and, besides, if I ever ran away, I'd want to take Snort with me — so I walk home from the bus stop with Abby.

I'm so scared that I don't even run when we pass by Zach. When I come inside, Mom gives me a what-have-you-done look. I have to explain everything to her, including how it was Jill's idea and how she blamed us for all of it.

"Lily," Mom tells me, "you will always have

friends with ideas; things that they want you to do or try. You need to listen to yourself. You know what is right and wrong. You need to make your own decisions."

"I know," I say.

"Then why did you do it?" she asks me.

"Because Jill makes everything sound like a good idea," I tell Mom.

"Well, maybe it's not such a good idea to spend time with Jill," Mom says.

"Yeah, maybe," I say.

I know she's right.

Chapter 23
The Nobody Club

I've made up my mind about what I'm going to do before I get to school the next morning.

"I'm quitting the Rizzlerunk Club," I tell Darby and Jill in the coatroom before class.

"No!" Darby says. "You can't quit. You're a founding member!"

"She can quit if she wants to," Jill says. "It was loads better as a two-person club anyway."

"Exactly," I say, looking at Jill.

"Please don't quit!" Darby says.

"I'm quitting," I say. I turn around and walk into the classroom.

I sit down and stare at my feet like I did at the beginning of the year. If I'm not friends with Darby or Jill, who am I going to be friends with? It feels like I'm starting school all over again.

I can hardly pay attention during math, but then during science we talk more about the life cycle of frogs, and it's pretty interesting.

"Frogs start out as one cell in an egg, just like humans do. Then the cell multiplies into two cells, then four cells, then eight, then sixteen. Can anyone guess how many cells they multiply into after that?"

"Thirty-two!" says Iris.

"Sixty-four!" says David.

"A googolplex!" says José.

"Okay, that's enough, children," Mrs. Larson says.

I think about Darby. She was just one cell. Was it a cell with bad eyesight? And Jill! How could Jill ever have been just one cell? I wonder if the one cell was mean. If it was, then when it multiplied, were all the new cells just as mean? Or is the first cell the meanest one in her body?

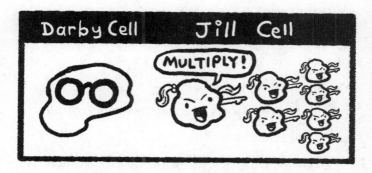

As Mrs. Larson tells us more about the frog life cycle, I start to realize how much humans are just like frogs! At first, we both look like tadpoles, and we both live in water, and then we both grow arms and legs and start breathing air. It's just that we start out on the insides of our moms, and frogs start outside their moms. It's definitely a lot more dangerous to be a frog.

The next thing I know, science is over and it's almost first recess, which means Darby and I are going to have to leave class for our first day in the RTC. When Mrs. Larson tells us to gather up our books, Jill actually looks like she wants to come with us — like she's jealous! Well, too bad for her. She could be coming, too, if she hadn't blamed us for her idea.

"Lily, I know you're mad at Jill for getting us into trouble," Darby says as we walk out of the room toward the RTC.

"She never stops getting us into trouble!" I say. "And she never will."

"I know, Lily. She's full of bad ideas, just like I told you. But, you know — we don't have to do them. And you definitely shouldn't quit the Rizzlerunks. It's our club. We can just tell Jill that she can't be the queen anymore, and we can stop doing whatever she says."

"Darby, if you could just stop doing what she tells you to do, wouldn't you have already done it a long time ago?"

"Probably," Darby admits.

"Then how can you still be friends with her?" I ask. "Why can't you just be friends with me, like it was before she came back from London?"

"I want to be friends with both of you!" Darby says. "Lily, Jill's been my friend forever. I can't just stop being friends with her."

"Well, then," I say, "I guess you'll just have to stop being friends with me, because I can't be friends with Jill anymore. My mom and dad told me that they think she's a bad influence."

We walk into the RTC, which is just a classroom at the end of the kindergarten hall with a few other naughty kids scattered around among the desks. I don't see any electroshock machines or anything, but I do see Mrs. 'Stache.

"Well, if it isn't the playground painters themselves!" she says with a sneer. "I knew your shenanigans would catch up with you soon enough. How nice to have the pleasure of spending some time with you."

We stand in the doorway, stunned, and look at her.

"SIT DOWN!" she says. "And as far away from each other as possible."

Well... BWAH HA HA HA!

I take one corner of the room in the back (as far from Mrs. 'Stache as possible). Darby takes the other corner. Mrs. 'Stache instructs us to take out paper and pencils.

"Now," Mrs. 'Stache tells us, "you will write a daily essay about what goes on inside your tiny little heads when you decide to make such preposterously stupid decisions, such as painting the playground bars and filling the boys' bathroom with jelly beads. I want details. And DO NOT make these short essays. You will be in here for five straight days. I will be checking your work every day. If I find your reasoning acceptable, I will sign your work at the end of the week and send it home to your parents, so they can understand what goes on in your tiny little heads, too."

We sit down and start writing. My pencil is dull and I want to sharpen it, because I hate writing with dull pencils, but I'm much too scared to ask Mrs. 'Stache if I can get up and use the pencil sharpener. Then, as she paces the room, she looks over my shoulder and gets mad at me for having such a dull pencil!

Finally the bell rings and we leave. Darby and I walk back to class together, but I walk behind her so we don't have to talk anymore, because my mind is made up.

At lunch, I decide to go to my safe place: the library. I pick out a book with lots of pictures. I should have known at the beginning of the year, when Darby was teasing me all the time, that I shouldn't be friends with her. I put my head down on my book. Why did Jill have to come back?

"Hi, Lily," I hear a voice say.

I turn and see Iris sitting on a beanbag behind me. "What are you doing here?" she asks me.

"Reading," I say.

"Why?"

"Because I don't have any friends anymore," I tell her. "That's why."

"Oh," Iris says. "What about Darby and Jill?"

"They keep getting me into trouble," I tell her.

"That's too bad," she says. "It seemed like you were good friends. I don't have any friends either, you know. It's not so bad, really."

Is she serious? I look at her. She looks serious. What am I supposed to say? Everyone has friends.

"I'm sorry," I say.

"It's okay," she says. "I get to read a lot. And I've made friends in the library, like Mr. Chan. He's a nice librarian. You know what? I don't think you have to worry anyway. They'll become your friends again soon."

"I don't want *them* as my friends," I say. "I just want Darby as my friend. I liked her better before Jill came back."

"Sure," says Iris. "I would if I were you, too. Darby acts different without Jill. I was in Ms.

Rock's class with her in second grade and Jill wasn't in there, so I know."

"Jill ruins everything," I say, "even the Rizzlerunk Club that we started together."

"Is your club named after Captain Rizzlerunk?" Iris asks me.

"You know about him?"

"Yes. Darby told me about him in second grade. It's such a strange story. But the truth . . ."

"Is stranger than fiction?" I finish.

"Exactly," she says. She smiles at me. "You can be in *my* club, if you like," Iris says.

"Really?" I ask her.

"Yes."

"What's it called?"

"The Nobody Club," she says. "I'm the only member."

"Oh," I say.

"When you're in it," she tells me, "it's like being invisible."

"I've always wanted to be invisible," I say.

"Join the club," she says.

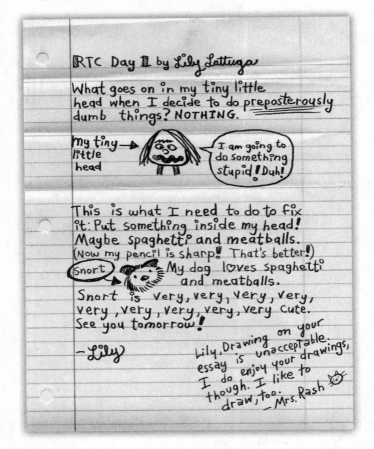

Chapter 24

Bad News Darby

The next morning I get on the bus with Abby, as usual, but this time Gabriella grabs my arm while I'm walking down the aisle and pulls me down next to her. Sonja and Tillie are in the seat behind us. I watch Abby go and sit next to a fifth-grader she doesn't even know. She's so brave.

"I heard you're not a Rizzlerunk anymore," Gabriella says.

"We were wondering if you want to join the Jilly Beans," Sonja says.

"It's more fun," Tillie tells me.

"Me?" I ask.

"Yeah, you," Gabriella says. "No one else is here."

"Oh," I say.

"Well?" asks Sonja.

"Jill and Darby would hate it," Tillie says, smiling.

This is my second invitation to a new club. I think Iris's invitation to the Nobody Club was supposed to be a joke, though. Hopefully, I won't hurt her feelings.

"Okay," I say.

We walk to class and hang up our coats together. When we walk into the classroom, Gabriella goes right up to Jill and Darby.

"Lily's a Jilly Bean now," she says.

They look at me. Darby looks worried.

"Right," Jill says. "Lily can do whatever she pleases. But I want my name back straightaway. You can be the Rizzlerunks."

"No, they can't!" Darby says.

"Yes, they can," Jill says. "It's a lame name anyway." Darby doesn't say anything, but she looks kind of sad.

"Fine, you can be the Jilly Beans," Gabriella says. "We're the Gabbys now."

"We're the cool club, you know," Gabriella tells us at recess. "They can have their Jilly Beans. They're like the vomit-flavored Bertie Bott's beans anyway."

"Yeah," says Sonja.

"Or the booger-flavored ones," says Tillie.

"Or earwax," I say, but I feel bad saying it. Everyone laughs.

I see Iris walk by. "Hi, Iris!" I say.

"Iris the virus!" shouts Tillie.

"You're not friends with her, are you?" asks Sonja.

"Uh . . ."

"Because if you're friends with her, you can forget being in the Gabbys with us."

"She is kind of weird," I say.

IRIS the VIRUS!

217

Now I have a terrible feeling in my stomach for saying Iris is weird. I mean, she is weird, but she's also really nice — in fact, she's nicer than all the other girls combined, except maybe Darby, before Jill came back. But if I'm friends with Iris, and Iris doesn't have any other friends — then I won't have any other friends either. I'm just happy to have friends again and be back in a club, so I keep quiet.

After school, Gabriella invites me to go to the Country Store with the Gabbys to buy candy. I don't really want to go. They make me uncomfortable. I decide to use Mom as an excuse.

"I can't go," I say. "My mom said that I have to call her if I want to go to the store after school, and I don't have a phone."

All three of the Gabbys hold out their phones. I call Mom.

"It's okay with me," Mom says, "as long as you don't eat very much candy."

I was hoping she'd say no.

At the Country Store, I'm overwhelmed by the choices in the candy aisle. Since I hardly ever get sugar, it feels like a huge decision to pick out a few pieces of candy. There are so many pretty colors of Jolly Ranchers to choose from! I'm trying to decide whether I like apple or cherry best when Darby and Jill walk in.

"Hi, Lily," Darby says.

I see Jill elbow Darby in the side.

I decide to pick both the apple and cherry Jolly Ranchers and put my Tootsie Roll back. I bring them up to the counter to buy them. I wave to Darby but don't say anything, since I don't want to talk to Jill. As I wait for the other Gabbys to buy their candy, I can't help but turn around to see what kind of candy Darby and Jill are choosing. I see Darby sneak a handful of Tootsie Rolls into her pocket!

What? I can't believe it! She's stealing! Darby wouldn't steal. Then Jill whispers something into her ear, and she reaches for a candy bar. Just as she puts it into her pocket, a man with a gray mustache walks out of the back room.

"Stop right there, young lady!" he says. "Show me what's in those pockets." Darby freezes. Then she starts crying.

"Oh, dear. I told her not to take it, sir," Jill says to the man in her most sweet-sounding British accent.

He gives Jill a look like he doesn't trust her. She turns her coat pockets inside out. There's nothing in them but a hair clip and her phone.

"I didn't mean to do it," Darby cries.

"You didn't mean to take the candy and put it into your pocket?" says the man.

"I mean . . . I'm sorry!" she says. "I'll buy them, and I'll never do it again! Please don't arrest me!"

All of us stare at them, but the store manager glares at us, so we leave.

What was Darby thinking? I guess Darby doesn't think when she's with Jill. Maybe I should go tell the store manager that it's Jill's fault.

"What was Darby thinking?" Gabriella says.

"That's what I was just wondering," I say.

"I *know*!" Tillie says. "How could she have been dumb enough to get caught?"

"What's that supposed to mean?" I ask.

"I mean," Tillie says, "she wasn't very quick. When you shoplift, you have to be quick."

"You've shoplifted?" I ask her.

"Yeah, haven't you?" Tillie asks me.

They all look at me. I shrug like maybe I have and maybe I haven't — but I just want to go home. I would never shoplift!

The next day at school Jill is telling everyone how Darby got caught shoplifting, and

Darby's laughing along with her, like she's proud of it!

"Did you get into trouble?" I ask Darby.

"What's it to you, Lily?" Jill says.

I walk out to recess with the Gabbys, even though I don't want to be with them anymore. I never heard of anyone stealing anything in my old school. I really don't want the Gabbys being mean to me, though, so I follow them to the playground.

"Let's play chase the boys!" Gabriella says.

I've never played that game before but I join in. We start running after Mikey, David, José, and Billy. Gabriella catches Mikey's shirt, then grabs him.

"Got you!" she says.

"Switch sides!" says Mikey.

The boys start chasing us. I can feel someone catching up to me. I turn around and it's Mikey. He catches me by the back of my pant leg and I fall down. "Sorry, Lily!" he says.

He puts out his hand and pulls me up from the

ground, smiling at me. He doesn't let go of my hand. I can feel my face getting hot.

"Mikey likes Lily! Mikey likes Lily!" the other boys shout together.

Gabriella spins around and glares at me. Sonja and Tillie glare at me, too. I drop Mikey's hand. Gabriella is the only one who's allowed to like Mikey. Everyone knows that.

"You are out of the Gabbys, Lily Lattuga!" Gabriella says.

They all turn around and walk away from me. The boys chase them. I'm so relieved that I can hardly breathe.

"Hi, Lily," Iris says from behind me.

"Hi, Iris," I say, surprised that she's out at recess and not in the library.

"Are you sure you don't want to join the Nobody Club?" she asks me.

"Thanks," I say. "That's really nice of you. But I think I'm done with clubs for a while."

"I understand," Iris says. "If I ever left the Nobody Club, I wouldn't want to join another club either."

I wonder how a person can leave a club when they're the only member, but I don't ask. We walk side by side back to class. We pass Darby and Jill, and I see Darby look at us, but she doesn't say anything. Jill doesn't even bother to look at us.

"Hey, Iris?" I say.

"Yes?"

"Even if I'm not in the Nobody Club, can we still be friends?"

"I'd like that," she says.

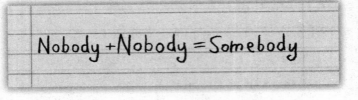

Nobody + Nobody = Somebody

Chapter 25
Frogball

On Saturday, I'm lower than low. It's raining, and I have nothing to do but watch TV or play with Abby. I watch TV. Then Mom tells me she has plenty of chores for me to do, so I ask Abby if she wants to go out in the boat.

"Let's catch frogs!" she says.

"That will make me miss Darby," I say.

"You'll be fine, Lily," Abby assures me. "You know what Dad says: if you fall off a camel, the best thing to do is get right back on the hump and ride."

Giddyup, Camel!

"You mean horse? If you fall off a horse, you get right back in the saddle and ride?"

"A camel would be more fun," Abby says. "Come on, maybe we can find some frogs' eggs and bring them to our end of the lake so we can finally have some frogs here to play with."

"Fine," I say. "I'll go with you."

We get a bucket, then put on our rain gear and get into the rowboat. I show Abby the bottom of Captain Rizzlerunk's island when we pass it and the top of the island at the park.

"That is literally impossible, Lily. Islands don't float. They're like mountains with just the top showing. All of Hawaii is made up of islands, and they just had a huge hurricane there. Do you think there would still be Hawaii if islands floated?"

"I know that!" I say. "I told that to Darby, but she swears it happened. Her dad told her it did!"

"Lily, her dad writes *ghost* stories!"

"I know," I say.

As we approach the end of the lake, we see there's a boat in the lily pads. It's raining so hard, we can barely see.

"Aww, someone else is catching frogs, too," Abby says. "I want all the frogs for us."

"It's fine, Abby. There are plenty of frogs to go around," I tell her.

I look at Abby and she's squinting into the rain, with her hand sheltering her eyes. "Isn't that Darby's raincoat?" she says.

I turn around and squint, and the rain jackets barely come into focus. The yellow one has black stripes on the sleeves, just like Darby's. The other one is black. It's Jill's.

"It's Darby and Jill," I say. "Let's go home."

"No way!" says Abby. "We rowed so far. I want to catch frogs! Come on, Lily, just because you're mad at them doesn't mean we can't go into the swamp."

"Fine," I say.

I start rowing through the lily pads, closer to Jill and Darby. "Hey!" Abby says. "What are they doing?"

"How would I know, Abby? I don't have eyes in the back of my head!"

"Well, turn around and look!" she says. "Is that Jill in the black coat?"

"Probably," I say.

"Lily! She's throwing frogs!"

"What?"

"I saw a frog flying through the air, so unless frogs fly, Jill's throwing them."

Then I see her do it. Jill throws another frog through the air.

 "Tell her to stop, Lily!" Abby says.

I'm too scared to tell Jill to stop doing anything. Where's my turtle shell? I just want to hide. I decide to pretend like I'm inside my shell with Abby and there's nothing we can do about it.

"No. I don't want to deal with Jill," I say. "She doesn't like me enough already. Let's just go back."

"No! Lily, she just threw two more. She's going to hurt the frogs!"

"Abby! I'm not going to tell Jill what to do!"

"Why? She tells you what to do," Abby says.

How does Abby know everything? I should tell Jill to stop, but I don't want her to be meaner to me than she already has been. Then I see a yellow arm with black stripes swing through the air.

"Darby threw a frog!" Abby shouts. "Do something, Lily!"

I can't believe it. Darby loves frogs. Darby is not thinking straight. Darby needs help. I need to get out of my shell—now! I row as quickly as I can toward them, cutting a path through the lily pads. I turn around and cup my hands around my mouth.

"Darby!" I shout. "DARBY! What are you DOING?"

Darby looks up at me. The rain lets up, and I can see her face. She stares straight at me like I'm one of her scary ghosts, then her face turns red and she bursts into tears. She's bawling.

Jill pulls her hood off and looks right at Darby. For the first time since she came back from London, I hear her speak without her accent.

"Darby! What is wrong with you? You are such a freak! Do you actually *like* the frogs?" Darby just cries louder.

"Fine, Darby, if you're going to be such a crybaby, I'll take you home. THANKS A LOT, LILY!" she screams at me.

"You know what, Jill?" I scream back. "Everything was better before you came back from stupid London with your stupid British accent and your stupid uniform and your stupid ideas that get everyone else in trouble. You're a bully. And you're a thief! You stole my friend just like you steal candy!"

"YOU'RE the thief!" Jill yells loudly enough that a bunch of frogs jump off the lily pads into the water. "You stole *my* friend! I got Darby first. I have dibs. She's mine and she does what I say, and I say she's never going to be your friend again. Right, Darby?"

I look at Darby, and she's crying too hard to say anything.

"So THERE!" Jill screams, and starts rowing away.

I don't care what Jill says. Maybe I can't save Darby — but at least I saved the frogs!

Chapter 26

Check Yes

Monday at school, I get a crumpled-up note passed to me by Iris. I can tell it's from Darby. Darby is the only one who crumples her notes up like garbage.

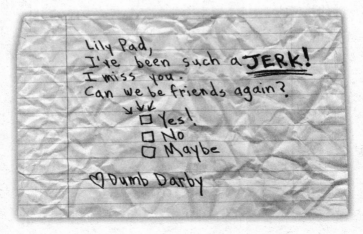

Lily Pad,
I've been such a <u>JERK!</u>
I miss you.
Can we be friends again?
☐ Yes!
☐ No
☐ Maybe

♡ Dumb Darby

I shove the note into my pocket. I'm not going to answer it. Darby was throwing frogs! Why would I want to be friends with someone who throws frogs?

At recess, I sit along the side of the building, where no one can see me. I look out at the playground and see Darby sitting alone by a tree. It looks like she's crying. She should be. She's a thief and a frog-thrower! I see Iris walking slowly toward Darby. She sits down next to her. For a while, they just sit there, leaning against the tree, then Iris puts her arm around Darby's shoulders. Darby starts crying even harder. She obviously feels terrible. But I don't care. Even if Jill made it seem like a brilliant idea, I wouldn't throw a frog! Would I? I think about all of Jill's brilliant ideas, and suddenly I'm not so sure.

Later, when we're doing a vocabulary sheet, I pull out Darby's note and uncrumple it. I read it again. Then I make a big red X.

Chapter 27

Five Hundred Frogs

Abby and I walk through the mud from the bus stop after school. After days, it's finally stopped raining, so we take off our hoods. We run across the slippery grass past Zach. Every time we go by, he jumps a little bit higher, which means he might jump over the fence one day. That would be bad.

When we get home, Mom's at work. All she left for us is a list of chores. It's so long.

Chore
list

I search through the refrigerator for something to eat. I find kale, almond milk, and condiments. I decide on the kale. I tear it from the stems like Mom taught me to do and put it into a bowl with some olive oil and salt. It's not Pop-Tarts, but it's not bad.

I look out the kitchen window at the lake. It looks like it's still raining over most of it, but the sun is shining on our dock.

I walk down to the lake to throw some sticks into the water for Snort. Abby comes with me. It's warm out, which feels so good. I throw the stick and Snort runs to the end of the dock and jumps off, flying through the air like a superdog and belly-flopping into the lake. Abby and I laugh. Snort gets out of the water, runs back onto the dock, and

SUPERSNORT

drops the stick at my feet. Then she shakes water all over us. I throw it again, and again she leaps from the dock and splashes into the water. Abby sits on the dock and looks out at the lake.

"This is the weirdest weather!" she says.

I look up. There's a huge fog bank still covering most of the lake.

"What if the rest of the lake is *gone*?" I say. "And we didn't even know it!"

"That would be like one of those old *Twilight Zone* episodes," Abby says.

I start singing the *Twilight Zone* music. *Do do do do, do do do do, da daaa!*

"Lily, look!" she says. "Out there in the fog!"

I think Abby's starting to make up an episode. But then I look up and see that there *is* something in the fog. Three boats are coming toward us: a pedal boat, a canoe, and a rowboat. The people on them are waving to us — and they're all wearing big round glasses.

"It's Darby!" Abby says.

"And Kyle and Katy and Deke!" I say.

When they get closer, I can hear them shouting our names. "Weewee! Weewee!" Deke yells. "Hi, Weewee!"

"That's the best nickname for you ever," Abby says.

"Don't *even*, Abby," I tell her with a sister glare.

When they get closer, I can see the boats have several buckets in them, and the floors of the boats are covered with something. Something moving—and hopping!

"We caught five hundred frogs!" Darby says, pulling up to the dock.

"Some will stay here for sure this time," Kyle tells us.

"I love froggies! I love froggies!" Katy shouts.

"Fwoggies fo' Weewee!" Deke says. "Fwoggies fo' Weewee!"

Darby grabs her bucket and steps out of her boat. She brings the bucket to the lawn and pours out all the frogs, then goes back for more. Soon everyone is helping get the frogs out of the boats. Snort is barking at them, but they aren't jumping away. Snort gets bored and starts playing with Deke, who is running around snorting like a pig.

After what seems like forever, all the frogs are on the shore.

"Look at them all!" I say. "There's no way they're leaving now!" Then we hear it.

MWAARP!

Everyone looks toward the sound, but the lake is still. We hear it again.

MWAARP!

Suddenly, there's a humongous splash. We see what looks like two enormous frog feet disappear into the water.

At that moment, all five hundred frogs begin leaping from the bulkhead into the lake.

"The bullfrog ghost scared them away!" Darby says.

"Stop, froggies!" Abby shouts.

"Stay here, froggies!" I say. "Please? It's not so bad here! I promise! In fact, I'm kind of liking it here!"

But the frogs don't listen to me. Every last one jumps into the water and swims away.

"That's the ghost I was telling you about!" Darby says to Deke.

"Dumb Dawby," Deke says. "Not ghost! It WEAL!"

"That had to have been the biggest bullfrog in the whole wide world!" Abby says.

"In the universe," says Kyle.

As the fog clears away, we watch the frogs swim toward Darby's end of the lake, like a giant black swamp monster creeping over the surface of the water.

After dinner, Abby and I turn on the TV to watch our favorite show. When it's over, Mom and Dad come and sit on the couch to watch the news. I take out my homework and start working on my math packet. Then I hear the announcer.

"And now, an incredible video clip sent to us by a boy named Mikey Frank, from Pine Lake, out in Issaquah," the man says.

I look up at the TV. Did he say Mikey Frank?

"This afternoon," the woman says, "a fourth-grade boy was flying his drone from the Pine

Lake Park dock and recorded this incredible video of an inexplicable mass migration of frogs swimming in the middle of the lake toward their usual habitat at the north end."

"Wow! Ample amphibians, aren't there, Susan?" the man says. "It looks like hundreds of frogs!"

"Those are *our* frogs!" Abby says.

"Yes, it looks like a boatload, Marty," says the woman.

"It was *three* boatloads!" I say.

"I don't think I'll be swimming in Pine Lake again anytime soon," says the man.

"Agreed. That is frog overload, Marty," the woman says. "But I am happy to see that the frog population is thriving in this favorite local lake."

"Now, hopping along with the news, Susan . . ."

I run to the phone and call Darby.

"Did you see the news?" I ask her.

"Yeah!" Darby says. "My mom was watching

it, and she called us all downstairs to see Pine Lake. She didn't believe me when I told her they were our frogs."

"It's amazing!" I say.

"It's totally FROGTASTIC!" says Darby.

Chapter 28

Democracy Rules!

When I come into class then next day, I look at Jill and, weirdness of all weird, she's not wearing her uniform. She's wearing regular clothes, like a regular girl. She looks up at me, and her eyes are all red, like she's been crying. Her face is wet, too. I think that she *has* been crying. I know I should ask her what's wrong, but I don't want to.

I don't care...
I don't care...

"Please take your seats, class," Mrs. Larson tells us. "It's time for SHTV."

"Shhhhh! TV!" everyone shouts.

Mrs. Larson gives us all her dramatic eye roll, then smiles and sits at her desk. I notice that Mikey's desk is empty, even though I saw his backpack in the coatroom.

There are two announcers on SHTV. I remember the fifth-grade boy from the first day of school. He looked so terrified on the first day, and now he looks relaxed. It must be costume day at SHTV.

After they announce the news and lunch (cheeze zombies — yay!), they bring on a special guest. It's Mikey!

"Exciting news, everybody!" says the announcer. "One of our own Sunny Hills students, fourth-grader Mikey Frank, made the local news last night when he caught some incredible footage of an unexplained migration of a whole lot of frogs on Pine Lake."

They cut to a clip of the video. "Mikey, can you tell us about how you caught the footage?"

"My dad and I were on the dock at Pine Lake Park with my drone," Mikey says. "We were flying it out over the lake . . . and I saw something that looked like a big black shadow-monster, sliding over the water! I flew my drone closer, and I could see it was a whole bunch of frogs! It was so weird, because all the frogs that I've ever seen on Pine Lake live in the swamp, so I don't know where they came from—maybe a giant frog swim meet or something, but I zoomed in closer and I didn't see any Speedos. My dad said he hadn't seen anything like it either, so we sent our video to the news—and they put it on TV!"

Darby raises her hand as soon as SHTV ends.

"Yes, Darby?" Mrs. Larson says.

"My brothers and my sister and I caught all those frogs to bring to Lily's house, so she could have frogs at her end of the lake, too. But a ginormous ghost bullfrog scared them all away!"

"What a creative story, Darby!" Mrs. Larson says. "It's perfect for your journal."

I can't believe I'm doing this, but I raise my hand. Maybe I'm not so supershy after all!

"Yes, Lily," Mrs. Larson says.

"Um . . ." I say, off to a terrific start speaking in front of the class. "It's true, Mrs. Larson. About the frogs. And the bullfrog. I mean, I don't know if it's a ghost, but it was huge, and it scared all those frogs away. I saw it happen!"

"Well, Lily, it sounds like you and Darby have a wonderful story to tell," she says. "How about you work together this morning as we write in our journals. Sound good?"

Darby and I have so much fun writing our

story. I know Mrs. Larson won't believe it, but we know it's true!

WHOA!

We have social studies next. We're studying the Revolutionary War, and today we're learning about the Stamp Act, which bossy King George III of England started. He wanted money from the colonists, so he told them that if they wanted to print something, they could only print it on his stamped paper. He taxed them for stuff like newspapers and playing cards — probably even comic books.

Mrs. Larson explains more.

"The colonists," she tells us, "got so angry that a bunch of them began to protest against the British. They called themselves the Sons of Liberty."

Then she tells us how the British wanted more money — so they started making the Americans drink only British tea! They called it the Tea Act. The Sons of Liberty were so mad that they jumped on one of the boats in Boston Harbor and dumped an entire shipful of tea into the water.

"Is Boston Harbor still made of tea?" asks Billy.

BLECH!

BOSTON HARBOR TEA

"No, Billy," says Mrs. Larson. "Boston Harbor is filled with salt water, and you most likely would not want to drink it."

When the bell rings for first recess and we go outside, I notice Jill walking by herself in front of us.

"What's wrong with Jill?" I ask Darby.

"I don't know," Darby says. "Either she's mad because we were saying bad stuff about the brilliant British, or she's mad at me. Yesterday I told her that she can't be the queen of the Rizzlerunk Club anymore. I told her that it was our club, and I'm president and she should have never taken it over. Then she quit. So I told her that I quit being her friend. I guess I'm having my own Revolutionary War! I'm the good guy, by the way."

Jill goes to the swing sets and sits on a swing, kind of slumped over. I actually feel sorry for her.

"Maybe we should go talk to her, Darby," I say. "She looks really sad."

"No way," Darby says. "She's just trying to get us to come over there so she can boss us around some more."

"Well, it's working," I say. "Come on, Darby, let's just make sure she's okay. She has been your friend since kindergarten, you know."

"Fine," Darby says, "but you do the talking."

We walk over to Jill and sit on the swings on either side of her. Darby starts swinging.

"Hi, Jill," I say.

"Hey, Lily," she says.

Where's her British accent? "Are you okay?" I ask her.

"No," she says. "I'm not okay."

"What's wrong?" I ask her.

"I'm moving back to London."

"What?" Darby says, skidding her feet on the ground to stop swinging.

"I'm moving back to London," Jill says. "My mom has to move back for her stupid work. I told her that I don't want to go, and she doesn't even care. She doesn't do what I say—she only does what her work says. I hate her work."

"But why don't you want to go?" Darby asks her. "I thought that it was so lovely and brilliant there. I thought it was so much better than here."

"I *hate* London," Jill says.

"What?" Darby and I both say at the same time.

"I didn't have one friend at my old school—and now I have to go back there."

"I thought you had ever so many friends," Darby says.

"Well, I exaggerated," says Jill. "Everyone there called me a bossy American, so I started speaking with a British accent—then they all teased me about that. At least I still knew that I had friends here. But now I don't have that, either. Everyone hates me—including you."

"I don't hate you," Darby says. "I'm just sick of you being the queen of me—bossing me around and getting me in trouble and everything. You're as bad as King George the Third!"

"Yeah, sure," Jill says. "I'm not the queen of you, Darby—it's obvious that Lily's the queen of you."

"Lily is not the queen of me, Jill," Darby says, her cheeks and nose getting red. "I'm the queen of me. Lily's the queen of Lily. And you know what? You should try being the queen of *you* sometime instead of everyone else! People would probably like you a lot more."

Darby gets off her swing. I get off my swing, too. "You can't leave!" Jill says, starting to cry again.

"We can do whatever we want to do, Jill," Darby says. "Why don't you try taking off your dumb queen crown and be a regular person like the rest of us?"

Jill looks at us with her watery blue eyes. A tear drips down her cheek. We turn around again.

"Wait!" she says.

We turn back toward Jill. She gets up from the swing.

"Darby and Lily, my lovely friends," she says, back to her British accent. "I shall removeth my crown. I am no longer the queen."

She pretends to take something off her head and put it on the ground.

We look at her.

"I submit!" she says.

Darby grabs my hand and raises it into the air.

"We are the Daughters of Liberty!" Darby shouts.

"Quite funny, Darby," Jill says. "Hey — is it okay if I bum around with you for the rest of recess?"

"Sure," says Darby. "Is that okay with you, Lily?"

"Sure," I say.

"So . . . what shall we do?" she asks us.

"We could play four square," I say.

"We could go to the invisible clubhouse," says Darby.

"I say, let's vote on it," Jill says.

Darby grabs Jill's hand and raises it into the air. "Democracy RULES!" Darby shouts.

"Lily, hold these sandwiches so they don't make a mess in the car," Mom tells me as I sit down next to Abby in Vanna.

We get to ride to school with Mom because it's Jill's last day, and we're having a good-bye party for her. Mom took over the job of class party planner (probably so she could make sure that we didn't get real treats during parties), so we're bringing the food and drinks. I helped her come up with the idea of a British tea party. We made little egg-salad and tuna sandwiches with cucumbers and colorful toothpicks. She also baked biscuits, but not the good kind that Jill had because Mom's don't have any sugar, of course. We can't make hot tea, so we're having cold tea instead. Mom even bought Jill a crown. I'm not so sure we should put a crown back onto Jill's head, but I guess it's okay for one day.

Darby and I are wearing the fake neckties and T-shirt vests that we made when Jill first came back. Lots of people in the class are planning to wear neckties to school, even Mrs. Larson.

When Mom and I get to the coatroom, Mikey opens the door for us since our hands are full. Mikey is wearing a red-and-green-striped necktie with a Santa Claus pattern.

"Oh, Mikey!" Mom says. "You look so handsome! Doesn't he look handsome, Lily?" I feel myself turning red. Mikey's face turns red, too. Gabriella, Sonja, and Tillie are standing in a circle adjusting their neckties, and Gabriella glares at me. I don't know why she thinks I like Mikey. Darby's the one with the crush on him!

When we get into the classroom, we all sit down and watch SHTV while Mom sets up the party in the back of the room. Mrs. Larson calls roll, then tells us that she has a special announcement.

"Not only are we having a lovely tea party hosted by Mrs. Lattuga," she begins, "but I have a big surprise for all of you, too!"

She walks to her desk, reaches underneath it, and pulls out two big boxy things covered in towels. She carries them to the front of the room.

"What are they?" asks David, getting out of his chair.

"David," says Mrs. Larson. "Seat."

David can't stay seated on a normal day! He runs to the front of the room and everyone else follows. David pulls the towel off one of the surprises.

"RATS!" shouts Darby.

Sure enough, there are two white rats in a

cage. Ethan pulls the towel off the other cage. Two more rats!

"Seats!" says Mrs. Larson. "SEATS!" We all run to our desks and sit down.

"Class," says Mrs. Larson, "with the help of these four rats, we will be doing a science project to learn about healthy eating."

"Healthy eating?" Mom says from the back of the room. "How wonderful!"

Science project? I thought we'd get to play with them. They're so cute! Their little pink noses twitch like someone who's about to sneeze, but they don't sneeze — their noses just keep on twitching.

*OK, they actually have little pink beady eyes, but they're still super-duper cute times one hundred.

"For our health unit," Mrs. Larson tells us, "we will be doing a long-term observation of the rats. We will feed two of the rats only junk food, like potato chips, sugared cereal, and soda. The other two will get healthy food, like nuts, lean meats, and grains. Then we will weigh and measure the rats daily and observe their activity levels."

Gabriella raises her hand. "Yes, Gabriella."

"Can we name them?" she asks.

"We can name them next week, when we officially start our science project," Mrs. Larson says. "Right now, I think it's teatime! Are we ready, Mrs. Lattuga?"

"We are READY to PAR-TAY!" says Mom.

MOM! Why does she say stuff like that?

Mrs. Larson puts the towels back over the rat cages. We all line up to get our sandwiches, biscuits, and tea. Jill is first, of course, and starts talking to Mom. She's back to her British accent.

"This is just lovely, Mrs. Lattuga. What a brilliant idea for a party!" she says.

I always feel uncomfortable around adults that I don't know, but Jill really knows how to make them like her. Jill stands between Darby and me as we eat. She pulls us close to her and whispers, "I have a brilliant idea!"

"NO!" I whisper back.

"NO!" says Darby.

"Let me at least tell you what it is before you say no," Jill says. "For the Rizzlerunks."

"Fine," we say.

She whispers in Darby's ear, then mine: "Let's let the rats out of their cages."

"NO!" Darby and I say together.

"Oh, Darby and Lily, you have to do it!" Jill says, pointing at her crown and smiling. "I'm the queen!"

"No way, Jill," I say. "We fought for our rights. As the Daughters of Liberty, we don't have to do anything we don't want to do!"

"Anyway, if it's such a brilliant idea," Darby says, "why don't you do it?"

"Fine. It's my idea. I'll do it," Jill says, surprising us.

Jill waits until no one is looking, then unlatches the rats' cages and leaves them a little bit ajar under the towels.

Jill walks away, and I keep watching the cages — but the rats aren't leaving. I thought rats were supposed to be smart! Then I see one peek its head out from under the towel, followed by another. The pair jumps off the table to the floor, like ninjas. Then two rats emerge from the other cage, their little noses twitching in the air. They scamper around the edge of the counter behind class projects and books.

"We'd better not get blamed for this," I whisper to Darby. Suddenly, Sonja screams and jumps up onto her chair.

"RATS!" she yells. "The rats are loose!"

A bunch of kids jump up onto their chairs, too, dropping their sandwiches on the floor. A rat runs right between Mrs. Larson's legs.

She screams. Then Tillie squats down to pick up her sandwich, and a rat runs right up her tights and under her skirt. She lets out a funny half-scream, then rolls back on her heels and faints, falling flat on the floor! The rat runs away.

"Tillie's dead!" Sonja yells.

"Oh, my goodness!" says Mom. "I'll go get the nurse."

I watch Mikey get out his cell phone and call someone, yelling into the phone about Tillie being dead. Mrs. Larson kneels next to Tillie, then runs over to the sink, gets a wet paper towel, and puts it on Tillie's forehead. Then another rat jumps from the counter onto the back of Gabriella's head. She shakes her head, and the rat starts to fall but grabs her ponytail and hangs on, flipping from side to side. Gabriella starts screaming louder than anyone I've ever heard. The rat drops from her ponytail, catches her sweater, then drops to the floor and scurries away. Gabriella keeps screaming.

Principal Walker, Nurse Feverfew, and Mom run into the room. Nurse Feverfew runs to Tillie, bends down over her, and starts checking her pulse. Tillie's eyes are open now, so she looks like she will live. Mom and Principal Walker surround Gabriella and try to get her to calm down.

"Make her stop!" David shouts, plugging his ears. "She sounds like a fire truck!"

"Isn't that a fire truck?" Iris asks.

It *is* a fire truck — a real one!

I look at Jill. She's sitting on her desk, smiling, like this is the best day of her life.

Suddenly, two firefighters run past our window, then burst into our classroom. I recognize one of them. It's Mikey's dad. That's who Mikey called!

The not-Mikey's-dad firefighter hurries to Tillie, who is definitely awake now but still lying on the floor.

Mikey's dad walks over and starts talking to Mrs. Larson. She's about to say something, but a rat runs right over her shoe and she screams, tips off of her shoe heel, and falls right into Mikey's dad, who catches her. She quickly stands up, straightens her skirt, and turns bright red. She looks like she has a crush on Mikey's dad!

I look over at Darby to see if she's watching Mrs. Larson, too, but she's busy clearing plates covered in half-eaten tea sandwiches and biscuits. She's stacking them in her arms like a waitress.

"What are you doing?" I ask Darby.

"Collecting food!" she says. "Help me!"

I start picking up plates, too. When Darby's arms are full, she sits down on the floor, her legs splayed in front of her, and dumps the food between them.

"Heeeeere, rat, rat, rat!" she says. "Heeeeere, rat, rat!"

She's calling the rats like we call the ducks! And they come! One after another, the rats run to the pile of sandwiches and start nibbling. She reaches down and picks one up.

"Put it in its cage, Lily!" she says.

I've never held a rat before, but I guess it's time to learn. I pretend like it's a frog, carry it to its cage, and shut the door.

"Here's another one!" Darby says.

One by one, I put the rats back into the cages.

"Thank you, Lily and Darby!" Mrs. Larson says. "Thank you!"

Mrs. Feverfew and the other firefighter each take Tillie by one arm and slowly lift her so she's standing. She looks all wobbly and pale. They walk her out of the room. Mikey's dad packs up their firefighter stuff, then walks over to Mrs. Larson. Now Mom's standing next to Mrs. Larson, and both of them are acting funny and turning red—like they both have a crush on Mikey's dad! I start blushing watching them. Luckily, he leaves.

As the door swings shut behind Mikey's dad,

Billy Snitch starts shouting, "Mrs. Larson! Mrs. Larson! You told me not to tell on people unless it's important. But this is important!"

"What is it, Billy?" Mrs. Larson says.

"I saw Jill open the cages, Mrs. Larson!" Billy shouts. "I SAW her!"

"Jill Johnson?" Mrs. Larson asks, as if there has to be another Jill, because this one certainly wouldn't do such a thing.

She looks at Jill. Jill shrugs and smiles. She looks at Principal Walker, who is still standing there.

"Jill Johnson, please gather your things and come with me," Principal Walker says.

As Jill walks out of the classroom, she drops a folded note onto my desk. I open it.

Hi, Lily,
Did you like Queen Jill's revolution? I simply HAD to go out with a =BANG!= BTW, it was absolutely brilliant being your friend!

Cheerio! ♡ Jill ♡

Chapter 30

The Endish

"What a sneaky rat Jill is!" Darby says to me after school as we walk to the bus together. "Having her own revolution."

"She left with a bang, just like she wanted, that's for sure," I say.

"Yep," Darby says. "It's too bad she had to go. Now I'll miss her all over again."

"I'll probably miss her, too," I say. "But I think we'll get in a lot less trouble with her on the other side of the ocean."

"I think you're right," Darby says, following me onto my bus.

We sit down and take out paper and pens to do heads and bodies.

"Let's send it to her in the mail," I say.

"She'll love it!" says Darby.

When we get to my stop, we grab our things and Abby follows us off the bus. We sprint past Zach, who's barking as wildly as Gabriella was screaming. He has big globs of slobber hanging from his mouth, catching the sunlight. It looks impressive. We get home and throw down our bags, then open the refrigerator.

We find a few leftover tea sandwiches and a biscuit.

"Let's eat them in honor of Jill," Darby says. "But we need real biscuits!"

We can't find anything close to a cookie, so

we spread butter on eighteen-grain bread and sprinkle chocolate chips on top.

"A biscuit!" I say. "Isn't it amazing how creative we are when we have nothing to work with?"

"To Jill!" Darby says.

"To Jill!" I say.

We wash it all down with some tomato juice and clear our dishes. Then Darby and I walk down to the edge of the lake, followed by Snort.

We sit down next to each other along the bulkhead and look across the lake. There's a warm breeze, and the sun is reflecting on the water like shiny diamonds.

"Remember the first time I came over?" Darby asks me.

"How could I forget?" I say. "Quack!"

"That seems like forever ago!" Darby says. "Way back when you were just a duck."

"Yeah, a lot has happened since then," I say. "Actually, I think I'm more of an amphibian than a duck now. Don't you?"

"Absolutely," Darby says. "I mean, it's like we

were just little pollywogs back then, and now we're grown-up frogs — with arms and legs and everything. It's metamorphotastic!"

Snort starts barking at a bush, so we get up to inspect what she's barking at. I can't believe what we find.

"One of the frogs you brought must have decided to stay!" I say. "Don't be shy, froggie!"

I pick up Snort, and the frog hops out from under the bush.

Then a second frog hops out behind it. Then two more!

"A family of frogs!" Darby says. "Four of them. It's just like your family!"

I bend over and look at the frogs.

"You are so brave, little froggies!" I say to

them. "You left your swamp just to come and live with me. And you know what? I think you're gonna like it here!"

One of the frogs croaks. Darby and I laugh.

"Now we just have to keep the big bully bullfrog ghost from scaring them away," Darby says.

As if on cue, we hear a rumbling *MWAARP* from across the lake. Then we actually see it for the first time. And it is huge—it's MONSTROUS! "It's as big as a mountain lion!" Darby says.

"It's as big as a whale!" I say. "No wonder all the froggies are too scared to live here."

The bullfrog takes a long leap from the shore. There's a huge splash and it disappears.

"That is one scary ghost frog," Darby says. "I'm telling my dad about that one."

"I don't think that's a ghost frog, Darby," I say. "That was the real thing. It was as real as Snort."

"Nah," Darby says. "Definitely a ghost. Anyway, dead or alive—it keeps coming back to haunt us."

"Just like Jill!" I say.

We look down and the four brave frogs are still sitting there. Then I look up at Darby — my still-newish bestest friend.

"You know what, Darby?" I say. "If we made it through the Ghost of Jill, we can get through anything together."

"Anything," she agrees.

"We're like superglue," I say.

"Yep," she says. "I'm the finger, and you're the forehead. We're stuck with each other!"

"Rizzlerunks forever," I say, doing a Rizzle Sizzle.

Szzzz

"Best buds, under frogs!" says Darby.

"With loyalty and honesty for all!" I finish.

And I mean it. Darby and I have already been through so much since we became friends — what else could happen?

How to Grow a Friend
by Lily

1. Find a seed.

2. Plant it.

3. Water it.

4. Feed it.

5. Talk to it.

6. Give it love.

How to Grow a Friend

by Lily

7. Watch it grow.

8. Dig it up.

9. Let it go.

10. If it comes back, it will be yours FOREVER!

A Bunch of Thanks

by Leslie

Thanks to my family and friends for making life seem like a comedy. Lucky me — I'm surrounded by people who turn life's ups and downs into hilarious stories.

Thanks to my parents, who, despite tearful protests, moved my sister and me to a beautiful little lake where we could live a life of outdoor adventure.

Thanks to my scientist sister, Gail, for inspiring Abby.

Thanks to my lifelong best friend, Di, who's as funny and full of fascinating (albeit questionable) stories as Darby.

Thanks to my other lifelong BFF, Michelle, whose witty sense of humor and devious ideas gave life to Jill.

Thanks to Ken, Mary Ellen, David, Cindy, and Jim Arasim for inspiring Darby's family and for having me around all those years.

Thanks to my agent, Rebecca Sherman, for getting me started on this project.

Thanks to my editor, Joan Powers, for guiding me through the process to finish it.

Thanks to Kristen Nobles and Lisa Rudden for the inspired art direction and design.

Thanks to Tatum Vontver for Darby's "bad" frog drawing; Addi Bevers for the lovely horse drawing; Marit Kaiser for crafting candy-wrapper bracelets; Mary and Amelia Krouse for reading the drafts; and many others who found themselves giving kid-input on demand.

Thanks to Scott Slonim at Hemingway Elementary School for the inspiration for SHTV.

Thanks to my husband and at-home editor, Jason,

for managing home and hearth when I'm locked in my (well-lit, second-floor) dungeon, writing and illustrating.

Thanks to my kids and additional at-home editors — Beck, Tia, and Tatum — who each passed through their own fourth-grade years, giving me first-hand insights into their own emotions and adventures at that age.

Lily finally feels settled at her new school, with her new best friend, Darby.

But when something happens to the class pet, Lily is caught in a lie. Can Lily find her way out of the lie that's threatening to get bigger and bigger?

Find out in . . .